Dead West

West of Pale

J Patrick Allen

Dead West: West of Pale
An 18thWall Productions book published by
arrangement with J Patrick Allen
verba mea in minibus
desiderium meum
Cover by Jason Behnke
Design by Elisgraphics

Series Editor: Nicole Petit

Table of Contents

Chapter 1

The Thing That Waits

Father woke me in the night with a hand clamped over my mouth. Through the shining moonlight I could see he was not looking at me, but rather out the window. In his other hand he held his Sharps buffalo rifle. Light and shadow threw contrast over his face, hiding his eyes but showing every nervous twitch of his jaw and beard.

"Get up," he whispered. I can still recall the spicy tobacco smell of his breath, the quivering fear in his voice. "No—slowly, son. Slowly, and keep low."

Following his instructions I slid out of bed on the far side of the window and hid behind it. Crouching, he led me away, backing up against the wardrobe. Outside I heard a snuffling, grunting noise. Some kind of animal, though what would make noises like that? The snuffling could have been an armadillo, but for the volume and depth of noise it produced. The grunting could have been a frog, but for the size of the sound. Whatever it was, it had to be the size of a man, and the thought put lead in my gut.

For a brief moment as the noise approached I feared I'd see something truly hideous appear at the window. I sunk a little lower behind the bed. During the day I might brag to the other boys of my bravery, but that was day and this was night.

According to the stories father told me the night time is the time for horrors. For packs of wolves out of the woods. For witches who roam the forest in their gingerbread houses, looking for disobedient children to eat. For fairies that make wicked bargains the mortal always regrets in the end. The night belongs to monsters.

The sound crossed around the corner, beyond the window and I felt father relax, a little. He motioned with his head for the wardrobe. Obeying I got in and he pushed me to the back, covering me with jackets and hung britches and shirts. For good measure he propped two open boxes of moth balls on the floor of the wardrobe.

Father rested a hand on my cheek, studying me by moonlight. "If I do not come for you by the morning, there is a secret compartment in the desk. Third of the small drawers, a false bottom."

"Yes, father." If he didn't come for me? Where would he be? Surely the animal could not get in the house.

"You are my son, Charlie." His voice broke at the end. I saw a single tear run a wet track down his cheek. He closed the wardrobe door and shut me into darkness. In with the smell of clothes, lye soap, and moth balls. In there, where the sound of my own frightened breathing almost drowned out the sound of him walking away.

A little light flared in the crack of the door. Father had lit a lamp. Just then the house shook. From above me a moth ball tumbled off a shelf and into my shoulder. I had to bite my hand not to scream.

Again the house rattled, and I realized what I was hearing. Something pounding the door. After a moment I heard the sound of glass shattering.

A new voice, gnarled and wheezy, shouted "You're mine, first born!"

Over my own labored breathing I heard the sound of father's Sharps fire. An animal roar pierced the night, followed by my father's own tortured screams. Just as suddenly as it started his screams were cut off. I heard something heavy—a body—drop to the floor, and something let out an asthmatic hiss.

That something was tumbled about the parlor. I heard furniture disturbed, glass knocked from shelves. And then it was over. I waited for father to come back. He never did.

When I could see the first rays of sunlight streaming between the wardrobe doors I pushed myself out. Cool morning air hit my face, and I could feel the air especially against my wet cheeks. I stumbled outside and behind the house. It was past the vegetable garden that I found the blood. The trail led off for the woods and the air carried a hint of the river stink of fish and urine.

My gut lurched at the smell and the sight of the blood. If there were anything in my stomach I might have lost it then. As it was I fell to my knees and retched. I spent several minutes there, my shoulders and gut clenching, waiting for the heaves to subside. When I was recovered enough I followed the trail like the crimson brush stroke of a gigantic painter.

The morning sun was not yet high enough to chase off the dark of the woods. Blue light mingled with black tree shadows and spots of dark mud. The morning birds were just beginning their song and somewhere distant a wood pecker hunted for breakfast.

Perhaps it was fear, perhaps it was the unusual situation I found myself in, but I felt eyes in those woods. My head cast this way and that, looking over my shoulder in search of the unseen watcher; all the while I kept an eye on the trail. The blood led to the muddy banks of the Missouri. The stain vanished among the rich dark mud, but a track dragged through it and down to the water. I found one of father's boots caught on a rock.

Numb, I walked home. My mind could not process what had happened. I like to believe it was shock. Whatever it was was sufficient to see me carried back to the house.

There, the constable and his boy awaited me.

"Little Charlie," he smiled to me. The constable's son Martin ignored me—we were not close.

I said nothing, and could say nothing. Something caught in my throat so I forced myself to nod in greeting.

"Where is Florian?" Constable Haak asked. I did not meet his eyes. He took stock of me—of the front door knocked off its hinges, of the broken window, and he nodded.

"I see. I'm here because Frau Blucher said there had been gunshots last night. Do you know anything about this?" He eyed the boot in my hand.

He waited, patient, while I found my voice. When at last it came to me I said, "Someone has killed him, sir." It was a small voice, quiet and gravelly. It hardly sounded like my own. "I followed the trail to the river."

"Do you know who did it?"

I shrugged, lost.

Constable Haak conducted a cursory investigation of the house. The smell of fish in the place caused Martin to blanch. The constable noted the disturbed living room, the bullet hole in the wall, and the discarded Sharps. After, he inspected the trail leading to the river. He said nothing to me, but I heard him a room over, conferring with his son.

“An animal,” he said. “It looks like an animal did this.”

I did not agree.

He found me a moment later, sitting on the edge of the bed I had shared with father, staring at the open wardrobe. Constable Haak laid a hand on my shoulder and told me of his findings.

Florian Kirchner, my father, was gone from this world. He had gone on to join the Father and I would not see him again until the end of my days. You must have some sympathy, as even one who is not a boy of thirteen would have done as I did. I turned and I cried. The Constable was kind enough to offer me his shoulder, and to offer to let me stay with him for a time. This was not the last offer I would receive. Behind his father I saw Martin frown. It was not the last offer I would turn down.

While he sat with me his boy went back on up the hill to town, and by the time the churches chimed noon local townswomen were stopping by to see to me. Each of course offered to let me stay with them until I could find my feet again. Frau Sackoff’s offer was the most tempting, as she ran a boarding house and I could have a space of my own instead of insinuating myself on another family—a happy family. And she was kind enough to help me when the mortician came to perform his bleak duties.

When evening came on I managed to urge the crowd that had formed in my father’s house to leave for the evening. And there I was, alone. I stared at a small picture of my father on the mantle place. He held mother’s hand. I do not remember much of her, but I had memorized the details of that photograph as I grew up. Now I turned my eye to him as well. He looked like me in so many ways. I had mother's long nose, but had inherited his sandy hair and brown eyes. When I felt like I could not look at the picture without crying again I turned away.

In that moment, in that time, the world ceased to seem rational. Along the bookshelves were a modest collection of science books, medical books, nature books—a legacy from Florian Kirchner, who wanted his son Charles to know the spiritual and literal wealth that knowledge could bring. The world was not rational. The world was a place of monsters. Father's words returned to me—the desk. I crossed the room to it and pulled out the third drawer. Turning the drawer bottom up I gave it three hard raps on the desk top. On the third knock the false bottom fell out and papers came with it.

Folded documents fell to the desk, scattering. It took me a moment of sifting through documents—the deed for the house, father and mother's immigration documents, a poem—to find what it was he must have been referring to. I unfolded a scrap of paper to find an unfamiliar man's angular, cramped writing.

thank you for the help
if your ever in trouble find this address & ask for Samuel Clayton
—SHC

The address listed was in Kentucky: Elizabethtown—place unfamiliar to me. It was something to think on. Why would my father recommend this Samuel Clayton to me? Who was this man, and why did I not know him myself? The name was obviously not German, so he would not be one of the towns folk. I tucked the letter and the address away in my pocket.

It was in my pocket that the papers stayed, through the funeral service the next day. It was at my bedside during the nights when I thought I could hear something stalking outside the house waiting for me (and a moment later it was with me in the wardrobe, hiding). And it was in my pocket when three days after I lost father I finally accepted Frau Sackoff's offer to let me stay at her boarding house.

I moved in to a small room at the top of her three story brick house, feeling safer even as I took a small bed in the corner of the attic. It's easy to feel afraid when you are alone and in the dark. It is much harder to feel afraid when you can feel and hear the presence of people about you.

That night I lay up, staring at the shifting shadows cast through the window by the moon and the trees. I thought I could hear something moving about outside, looking for me. Waiting for me. It stalked circles about the house for perhaps a few hours until I heard it no longer.

When the noise ended my pulse returned. I withdrew the note from the pocket of my trousers, which were hanging on the back of a chair and read through it for the hundredth time. The way I saw it, I had two choices: stay here and wait to be pulled into the river, or find the man who wrote this letter.

Really, there was only one choice.

Chapter 2

The Midnight Ride

I consider it a special kind of madness that had me leaving the house that night, despite fears of something stalking me. Mania and curiosity mashed into a slurry of dread and a sense of looming mortality. Still, I had my head on enough to be considerate: I left money on the dining room table where Frau Sackoff would find it. Some little compensation for what I was about to steal.

A dime novel might have had me running off into the night astride a great hulking black beast of a horse, but truthfully the only thing I felt comfortable taking from the stable was a mule that Frau Sackoff occasionally used for pulling her buckboard. I saddled it and disappeared, hopefully to return triumphant and avenged of Father's death.

A road followed alongside the river, connecting the various scattered communities of the Missouri Rhineland. This was the path I took on that clear and cold late March night. I traveled simply, with only the clothes on my back and with the Sharps across the saddle. Now today you don't often see a Sharps rifle, or many buffalo guns at all since those beasts have been all but driven to extinction. But let me tell you about that rifle. It was nearly as long as I was tall, well darkened with age, with the soft angles and curves of a beautiful dancing woman.

Guns were a work of art back then. Our rifle in particular was an old soul even when Father purchased it—a smoothbore, which was an oddity even back then. But that simply meant a poor German immigrant could get a good price on a tool to scare up a little meat for the dinner table. It could only hold one round and was a chore to load, but if you had a steady hand you could tag a critter from a tremendous distance. All you needed was one shot.

I'd taken a blanket for a bedroll and a few days' worth of food. Father had taught me to shoot, so I thought I'd hunt up some meat when Frau Sackoff's biscuits and jerky started to run low.

When the road began to drift away from the river I felt a knot loose itself in my chest. A scattering of maple and sycamore blocked the river from view though I could still hear the flow, still smell the fishy river mud churned up by spring rains along the banks.

A waxing quarter moon provided all the light I needed that night, and it was well into the sky when the tense sensation of eyes returned. I cast my eyes over my shoulder, seeing only the dark shadows of grass and trees crowding over the road.

A woman's scream broke the night air.

My blood froze. A moment after, the mule stopped and I realized that I had a strangling grip on his reins. A moment later I realized the sound was nothing more than the cry of a fox. Somewhere out there beyond what I could see a farmer was losing chickens. But at least it wasn't the monster.

The mule blew a snort of air, tossing its head in complaint of the brief run. I caught my breath and laughed. "I'm most sorry about that, Mr. Mule. I thought there was a monster on our trail."

Lights appeared as we rounded the bend of a hill. A small farm where someone in the house was up even at this time of night. I could just make the vague shapes of grape vines. A fence ran right up to the road, and just behind it a pair of cows drank at a small pond.

A warm place to sleep, even a hay loft, sounded wonderful. On the other hand, a boy showing up in the middle of the night only a few miles from town was sure to elicit comment. And the name of Florian Kirchner was well known. I would be recognized. For a moment I wondered if perhaps it was time to find a place to camp.

I began to let the farm disappear behind me when I heard the cows. The lowed, disturbed, and the sound of splashing water carried across the night air to me. I turned, slowing the mule.

There, by the light of the moon, I first saw it.

A bulbous shape like a man with two arms and legs, yet unlike a man in proportion, clambered over the fence and shambled into the road. Its eyes flashed, catching moonlight and I knew they were watching me.

My ears strained for any sound they could grasp. It was for that reason that I caught the words it spoke. "I thought I had smelt a boy-child in that house."

The mule danced sideways, likely sensing something was amiss. That was when the shape squatted low and sprang into the air. The jump handily ate ten feet and converged on me.

"G'yap!" I whipped the reins, but Mr. Mule needed no prompting. It took off down the road, screaming terror and nearly bucking me off. The gun rattled in my lap and I almost lost it.

We turned a corner and the path widened into a traveled road, ditches on either side. Checking behind me, I knew it was still there. Trees created pools of black, cut only by where the moon turned the packed dirt white. The shape would vanish into those pools and then leap out again, suddenly much closer. With each leap it hissed and spat.

"Kirchner!" it cried in a strangled, playful voice. "Give me what is owed!"

I screamed and the mule bolted just ahead of the creature's webbed, clawed fingers. Behind me I saw the creature rear up like it was taking a deep breath. I don't know if it was instinct or some quiet warning voice, but I ducked. I felt more than saw the long, barbed tongue fly past my ear.

I looked over my shoulder to see the dark form drop to fours and leap again into the air. It cleared ten, perhaps fifteen feet and then again with another leap. I whipped my reins harder. The mule brayed a scream and tried to jerk them from my hands.

It caught an overhead branch mid-leap and rather than plowing toward me it dropped into the ditch to one side of the road. I heard a splash of water deeper than I would have guessed the ditch held. I hardly had time to think about what I'd seen before the creature burst from the water in the opposite ditch, ahead of us.

We were faster, but just. As we shot past it, the creature cursed at me and in another leap grabbed onto the mule's hind. The smell of river water, fish, and rotting meat was overwhelming. Mr. Mule bucked onto its front hooves and kicked with the back. I heard the sound of cracking bones as I was nearly pitched over the front of my saddle.

Regaining my seat, if just, I looked back over my shoulder. The figure lay in a pool of moonlight, still. Quickly it was carried out of view by a shifting of cloud and tree cover, and by our own hasty retreat.

I sucked in a shuddering breath and exhaled with a moan. My hands shook and I didn't trust myself to really control the mule's path. Smartly, it continued along the road and slowed after a mile or two. When I could think again I stared at the ditches to either side of us. They could not be connected. How had the thing done that trick?

"It hides in water."

Four hours to dawn I finally trusted myself to make camp—well away from water—and slept until first light. The midnight run carried me further than I'd figured on going in one night, and to my surprise I was in St. Louis by late afternoon the next day.

Chapter 3

Elizabethtown

I thought about catching a boat down the Mississippi but the cost was beyond my means. Rather I crossed the river, and over the next few weeks I made my way east and south (though mainly east) to Elizabethtown, Kentucky.

A month gone from Hermann, the appearance of the place tugged a string of homesickness in my chest. Red brick buildings and fine homes washed in white spread across gently rolling wooded hills sad beside the thin dark blue vein of a river. I arrived mid-morning in early April, the warm clear sky hatched with streamers of stove smoke. All around, the trees were already showing their green and the flowering ones had long since begun to rain pink or white petals on the street.

I still stayed clear of the river, and looked askance at any pond or creek I encountered. A boy of thirteen riding a mule, dirty from travel, and bearing an ancient Sharps slung across his shoulder warranted a few glances from the people of the town, but I was left to my devices.

I rode down the street, taking the town in. I'd seen much like it on the journey, but it was one of the larger towns I'd crossed between Missouri, Illinois, and Kentucky. I passed by a hotel, peering in the windows. Just on the other side of the glass I could see men and women being served eggs and toast, or warm bowls of grits or oatmeal. One gentleman was tucking into an enormous plate of hotcakes. My mouth flooded with saliva and I pulled up short.

I must have been caught staring, because a few moments later I heard a voice nearby. "You got money to pay, or are you going to stare at my customers?"

I jumped, falling out of my daydreams of hotcakes and sausage and turned to the speaker. A rotund woman in a striped dress with a messy bun of hair wiped floured hands on her breakfast-stained apron.

"Oh, I am sorry," I stammered. My English had improved since leaving home, but the accent was still thick as molasses. "I have just arrived in town, and…"

The woman smiled softly. "All by your lonesome?"

I ducked my head, looking down. "Ah, yes ma'am."

"A little young to be traveling." She eyed the rifle. "Well you look famished. Come in and sit a spell. I'll only charge you for the coffee, how's that sound?"

On my limited funding it sounded like heaven. The biscuits and jerky had gone a week and a half ago, and I didn't seem to have much luck hunting. Seemed the animals always spooked just before I pulled the trigger, or else I missed.

I tied up my mule at the nearest hitching post and gathered my things, walking inside. A man at the front desk glared at my filthy appearance until I wiped my feet on the rug. At that he simply sniffed and ignored me. The next room was the hotel's saloon, lobby, and café all in one. The wide woman with the apron was waiting for me with a small table set in the far back corner. A table for one, more a wine barrel with a spare table top and tablecloth draped over it.

"What will you have, sugar?" she asked as I came over. "You can have anything in the house. Just don't abuse the kindness or I'll make you pay, hear?" She gave me a wink that made fire bloom in my cheeks.

Rather than coffee she came back with a gigantic glass of milk. It was fresh too, still warm. I savored the taste as I gulped it down. Before long she came back with a plate of flapjacks and bacon the milk was gone.

"Liked that, eh?" She laughed. "I'll bring another."

I tucked into the food while she went to fetch another glass. The flapjacks were hot, smothered in melting butter and caked with ginger and brown sugar. Each bite danced in my mouth and when she handed me another glass I immediately bolted down half of it just to clear my throat.

When the woman walked away again my thoughts turned, and the pace of my eating slowed. I munched the crispy bacon, occasionally smearing a bit in the brown sugar before popping it in my mouth. First order of business would be to track down the address on the paper, and this mysterious Samuel Clayton.

No, maybe first business would be a bath. I knew I smelled, and my pants could probably stand on their own. But maybe the monster could come from a tub of wash water? The best I could hope for was a used tub of water, so I'd never even see the river-thing before it jumped out at me. Even if money weren't an issue, it felt like a bad idea. And of course bathing in the river or a pond was right out. I shivered at the thought.

I'd just stink.

When I'd finished eating the woman came back, collecting my plates. "So you traveled a piece, huh?"

I nodded, not daring to say anything. My own accent sounded foolish to my ears now that I was beyond the Missouri river valley.

"Passing through, or coming here in particular?"

"Coming here," I sounded the words very carefully. I made a promise to myself that I would wipe my accent as fast as I could. "I am looking for an address."

At that I reached into the pocket of my britches and pulled out the now wrinkled piece of paper. She accepted the note, balancing the dirty plates in her arm, and gave it a quick glance. After a moment her face darkened.

"I'm afraid I don't recognize the name of the man you're looking for," she said without a trace of her former sweetness. "I've taken your dishes. Just leave your money on the table. I think it best you be on."

The sudden shift in demeanor stunned me. "But…"

She handed back the paper and turned her back to me, marching for the kitchen. I knew that look. It was the look I'd seen on the faces of my old friends and neighbors back home. It was a look of suspicion, of a doubt that I was even human. With my heart sunk into my belly I paid for my meal and collected my things, leaving.

At least said belly was full. The sudden turn in disposition stung, but it could have been worse. Mr. Mule and I walked up the street asking about Samuel Clayton, and at each turn the faces turned dark and scowled. One man with a crutch and a long beard even tried to hit me with the crutch. People walking out of the restaurant were already eyeing me askance before I even came up to them. I supposed the woman there must have already talked.

Whatever Samuel Clayton had done or whomever he was, he wasn't well liked here. I decided to try the next street down, and a different tack.

The first woman I encountered, walking to a dry goods store, stopped as I came up to her.

"Excuse me, could you tell me—" I checked the address on the letter. "Could you tell me where the old parish road is?" I paid special mind to my consonants, trying to sound like one of the locals.

The woman seemed suspicious regardless. She eyed my filthy appearance, the mule, even my long gun, though she did nothing but smile. "Of course, darling. Go up here and take a left on Elm. Follow it south out of town. The old parish road is a few miles south."

I doffed my hat and gave a mumbled thanks. At last—progress.

The road out of town took me through the woods and hills. Plots of land were cleared away for farms, though in several instances the farms were still over-grown ruins left over from a war not three or four years done. Some of the farms were new built and from time to time I'd see a man here and there, white or colored, driving a plough or otherwise preparing his fields for spring.

The old parish road took a dark turn between two taller hills. The woods here were cool and dark, the air smelling of deadfall and dew on rock. And to my relief they took a turn away from the river.

The tree cover parted and I came upon a clearing that had once been a wide field. Nearer to the road sat a house of diminished grandeur. Once it might have been shining pristine white, but now the whitewash was faded, revealing silvered wood and red brick. Curtains were drawn over the house, though not much sunlight might get in due to the massive oak trees standing sentinel over the property. I walked up the short lane which passed by the big house on the way to a carriage house. On the far side of the field I could see the burned out remains of buildings—likely slave housing.

I tied up Mr. Mule at the carriage house and walked the circumference of the house. At first the only sounds were of wind rustling the leaves and of the mid-morning spring birds. Off in the distance someone's hound brayed. By all appearances the place seemed abandoned, but maintained. The curtains were shut all around and the chimneys gave no smoke. Ankle length grass grew right up to the porch wrapping around the building, and the eaves were starting to fill with bird nests.

When at last I found myself back at the front of the building and tried the door. I used the huge tarnished brass knocker, shaped as a lion, and waited. At a mental count of thirty I tried again. When a few minutes passed, again.

Nothing.

I tried the door, which to my expectance, was locked. I stood back, peering through the gaps in the window curtains. My heart caught a moment, half expecting the river thing to rush at me from the dark inside. But nothing happened. All I saw were the barely lit shapes of furniture covered in tarpaulin and bed sheets. There was a dusty sort of opulence to what few furnishings and paintings were visible.

"Ain't nobody home, mister."

I gasped, spinning on my heels to face the owner of the voice. A colored man in homespun and a straw hat came up the lane fanning himself with the collar of his shirt. His skin glistened with sweat from an already long morning at work in the fields.

"You lookin' for Mister Clayton?"

My hands clenched nervously, itching for the Sharps rifle I'd left with the mule. He stared at me, expecting, saying nothing. Finally I nodded.

"Well he ain't here."

"Do you—ah—" I cleared my throat. "Do you work for him?"

The man came up the drive, and I could see his shaggy hair was starting to develop touches of grey. Deep wrinkles carved a map on his face. He sniffed as he inspected me in all my filthiness. "Not for pay, no. Ah, no don't make that face. T'ain't like that. 'Specially not after the war. I tend to his house while he gone. I suspect you know Mister Clayton is gone most the year."

I shook my head, feeling my heart sink. "I didn't know."

The man smiled sadly. "You one of them, ain't you?"

"One of what?"

"You need his help. I needed his help once."

I tilted my head, frowning. "With what? What kind of help does Mister Clayton give?"

The man scratched as his beard, considering me for a moment. While he mulled me over I pulled the now-crumpled note and showed it to him. That gave him something further to think over.

"This's his handwriting alright. Samuel Henry Clayton." He tapped the initials at the bottom of the paper.

“What kind of help does he offer?” I asked again. “I am in a bind and—”

“Tut-tut now, son. We don’t talk ‘bout the help Mister Clayton offers. His purview be things beyond the pale. People who talk too loudly ‘bout that invite trouble. You mention him on your way in?”

I frowned. “I did. What does *beyond the pale* mean?”

He didn’t answer my question. “Best you avoid the town on your way out then.”

“But what do I do? If he is not here—sir, I am being—”

He threw up his hands warding me off. “Whoah, whoah. I don’t know what you being, an’ I don’t need to know. That’s trouble for sure. You want Samuel Henry Clayton that bad? Lemme tell you. Last he told me, he was bound for Iowa.”

I watched him for a moment before speaking. He met my gaze, scratching at his beard.

“Did he say where in Iowa?” It was a big place, after all.

“Muscadine or something like, if’n I recall. He got a letter from an acquaintance. It’s along that Iowa river.”

“Muscadine, Iowa,” I said to commit the name to memory. “Muscadine, Iowa. Thank you.”

“You tell him Samson say hey.”

“I will. Thank you.”

We said our goodbyes and I made my way back toward Elizabethtown. As I passed the main drag I saw a small crowd gathering, some of them bearing rifles and looking none-too-friendly. I turned the mule and made myself scarce, finding my way back north alongside roads. With a heavy heart I resigned myself to more travel and sleep on the ground. And an empty stomach.

Chapter 4

Caduceus

For the trip north, as with how much of the journey went, my nights were often sleepless. I huddled, paranoid, close to the fire with the buffalo gun in hand. Or alternately I would spend the time crying like the fool child I was over the loss of my father. Often I would find myself replaying the events of that destined night, in which I burst from the closet and snatched the rifle off the mantle (where Father in the real course of events had already taken it from), shooting the water-thing between its bulging yellow eyes.

This was idle foolishness, naturally. In an existence where each precious bullet potentially meant the difference between a full belly and an empty one, my marksmanship had improved some but not nearly enough. Passing through St. Louis on my way north I spent the last of my little cash left. I'd had to choose between jerky for the road or the sundries needed to load the Sharps. In the end, I split the difference between the two and on the nights that I missed I ate the jerky.

Which is to say the first few nights I dined on jerky. For a few weeks after that I would be hungry.

When I stopped in St. Louis I asked about Muscadine, Iowa. None knew the name. Regardless I continued my way north along the Mississippi. I stopped only long enough at the confluence of the Mississippi and the Missouri to stare along the Missouri and think of home. The night after I passed the confluence was a rough one for home-sickness.

At a ferry crossing I asked again about Muscadine. The man running the ferry rolled his mustache between his thumb and his forefinger, thinking the word over aloud.

"No, son. Don't know no Muscadine. There's a Musca*tine*, though. It's in Iowa country north of here. Ain't on the Iowa, though. It's along this here Mississip."

It was enough of a lead. I made my way along the river, stopping only when the sun began to go down at night and after I'd made sure each evening that I was well away from the river. That damned river. There was no place I could be that was far enough away from water. Along the journey I'd heard men back from the west talk of great expanses of nothing but sand and brush. That sounded preferable. Perhaps if I never found this Samuel Clayton I would go west.

In the lonely times I talked to the mule. At first I conversed in German, my most familiar tongue. Eventually however I realized it was for the best that I become better acquainted with English. I knew the language, and I could read it fluently, but my tongue still wagged with rolled Rs and misshapen Ws.

There were no more close calls along the river. Eventually even my hackles ceased to rise when I got too near the water. I found a small creek to wash up in one afternoon. I smelled bad enough that even I could not stand myself, so the chance to wash the mud off my clothes and the stink off my body was welcome.

I still did not sleep anywhere within two miles of running water if I could help it, and the dark always brought the fear back.

Weeks after I'd left Elizabethtown, I forded the Iowa river where it met the Mississippi and the next day I was in Muscatine. The road became wider, flatter, and more trampled as I rode. Farms became more common, and soon I passed the first outlying buildings of the town. Great river boats crowded the shore along town loading or unloading their cargos and passengers. Even from miles off I could see the plumes of their smoke stacks in the sky.

The town was bustling, perhaps a little larger than Hermann, and with an active population. Where home was hilly, defined by vertical spaces and grassy climbs, Muscatine was spread out over a more level land. Where the countryside back home was defined by vineyards and farms separated by expanses of old woods, Muscatine was open to the sun. Even the air carried a sharper, dryer quality to it.

I asked around regarding Samuel Clayton. Some said the name sounded familiar, but could not recall anything. A few times I asked about his full name. That got some traction.

"How about Samuel Henry Clayton?" The man I spoke to ran the dry goods store and a post office.

He tapped his pipe against the wooden counter and stared at the rafters where pelts and jerky hung. "Let me check my book."

A moment later he returned with a thick ledger. "No Samuel, but here…six weeks ago, a Henry Clay received a package from Boston. And here—shipped a package to Boston. Log says he was staying in Amana."

"What's Amana?"

He looked at me over the rim of his spectacles, a slightly surprised look creasing his brows. “I figured you for one’a them. German folk.”

“Germans?” My head popped up and my breath caught.

“Yessir. Popped up here a few years ago. Down along the Iowa. Follow the road out’a here going west.”

“I will. Thank you sir!” I turned for the door. I had no money to give the man, else I’d have bought something for his trouble.

“Careful of them, son. They’s pious folk.”

I glanced over my shoulder, receiving the words as I stepped out onto the crowded street.

Amana was a small patch of German paradise in the midst of the Iowa wilderness.

The surrounding countryside was often flat but for the occasional roll or rise of a hill. At each farm I saw men hard at work, children seeing to chores, and mothers herding chickens with an apron or churning butter on the porch. Tall red and white barns dominated vast fields already showing the first signs of spring wheat or corn.

The town itself sat on its own tall slope of land overlooking the surrounding farms. There was not much here yet, a handful of stores and a restaurant, each built in the familiar exposed-frame style. The red brick walls of a church were going up next to the wooden walls of a more makeshift place of worship. There was a hint of saw-dust in the air—everything smelled *new.*

There was perhaps fifty people living on the hill among the houses and businesses, but where they gathered and talked I heard the glorious consonants of my own language.

They eyed me suspiciously, but I was too happy to hear their voices. I'd nod my head or tip my father's hat and give them a "Good afternoon," or a simple "Hello, how are you?"

The words drew some surprised looks, and eventually I was stopped by a young couple at a new-built house not even whitewashed yet. Hanging from the eve of the porch was a wrought-iron *Caduceus*. Twin snakes entwined as a staff—a doctor's house. I thought again of Father and of the plans we had made for my future.

"You seem young to be traveling on your own," the husband said.

"I am looking for someone, and was told he had come here."

The wife was bouncing a little baby girl on her hip with one arm and shielding her eyes against the sun with the other. "A great many people are coming here. We all come west."

I nodded. "Yes. My father and mother brought me out west when I was a baby. Though I was born in Boston shortly after they arrived."

The wife laughed. "You are a true American then, like our little Elisa." She looked down at her baby giving her a radiant, affectionate smile.

"Where are you from?" the husband asked. He removed his spectacles and whipped a handkerchief from his waistcoat pocket to clean them.

"South of here, in Missouri. Hermann."

They glanced at each other and for the first time I had a bad notion about this beautiful new town. There was something in the glance they shared.

The husband laid an arm across his wife's shoulder. "Would you excuse us for a moment, Herr Kirchner?"

I nodded and he led her toward their front door, conferring. After a moment he returned, wringing his hands. "Herr Kirchner, we would be remiss if we did not offer a hungry and road-tired looking young man like you a place to eat and stay for the night. Please, come in."

Something in the quiet urgency underlining his polite words set my teeth on edge. But I accepted, leading Mr. Mule to the back of their house and unsaddling him and brushing him down to rest beside their lone horse and buck wagon. The wife brought me in through the back door which opened on a small kitchen dominated by a pot belly cook stove. Fresh bread cooled on the open windowsill beneath white linen napkins, filling the room with their scent.

"I am Edda Steiner," she said, giving a curtsy.

Herr Steiner entered from the dining room carrying the baby. "And I am Doktor Ludolph Steiner. And *this* darling as you know," he said holding propping up the baby, "is little Elisa Steiner, and she is our joy."

They led me into the dining room. Something worried hid behind their smiles, but Frau Steiner still offered me a glass of milk and a plate of sausage and a hunk of cheese. After, they would offer me some cookies ("Herr Steiner likes sweets too much, and I am too good a wife not to say yes to him." They laughed). But while I devoured the sausage they watched me.

Finally as I paused in eating Doktor Steiner realized he must explain himself. "Herr Kirchner, are you Lutheran or Catholic?"

I hesitated. "Lutheran. Why?" I answered readily, though truthfully I had left shortly before completing confirmation.

They glanced at each other. "We are Lutherans as well, of a sort. Pietists, to be precise. Though many Pietists are distrustful of our Lutheran Brothers in Christ and the Catholic heretics for the persecution they have made our people suffer."

I nodded. Growing up in America it had never been a fact of life for my father and I, so I was unfamiliar with the particulars of what they relayed to me. But it still left a question in my mind.

"If you're distrustful of me…" My eating came to a stop and I regarded the plate, worried.

"Frau Steiner and I believe one of the Christ's first commandments was to love our enemies as our self, and to treat others as we would like to be treated. You seem a kind boy, and we wanted to bring you in off the street before you divulged yourself to someone who would be less…" He glanced at his wife and his babe, making a helpless gesture with his hands. "Charitable."

The house was small. The dining room and sitting room were one in the same, divided only by the stairs that took you to the second story. They sat me in a winged back chair while she continued to offer me cookies. After a time baby Elisa began to fuss so Edda took her and wandered up stairs to put her down to nap.

Doktor Steiner took out his pipe and began cleaning it. "When we met you said you were looking for someone."

"This is true," I said.

"Is he family? What was his name?"

I shook my head. “He is apparently a friend of my father’s. His name is Samuel Clayton.”

The doctor tapped a bit of tobacco into the bowl and paused, thinking. “No, I do not believe I have heard the name.”

“Henry Clay perhaps?”

He shook his head and walked into the kitchen to light his pipe from the stove fire. After a moment he returned and puffed at the pipe. When the smoke was running nice and thick and finally said, “No, I do not believe I know of any such man who has come through Amana.”

To the doctor’s surprise—and to mine too—I sniffled. That was the crack that preceded the dam’s break. My eyes began to burn and soon I lost all sight but light and colors to the tears swimming in my eyes. I clamped them shut and curled in on myself.

“My dear boy, what is the problem?” He was to my side almost immediately, laying a hand on my back.

But I couldn’t speak, not for several minutes. Weeks of pent up frustration came uncoiling at the news that I had lost him. How could he help me now? How could he have even helped me before? Who was he? All these would remain unanswered now.

I saw a short future ahead of me. I could return to Hermann, perhaps. But surely the river-thing would be waiting for me. My mind brought forth the images of that blood sprinkled trail through the field and the woods, running into the river. I imagined the creature dragging me, unwilling, into the water. I could hear the sound of the water closing over my ears. I could taste the cold gritty flavor of the Missouri. I knew how it would end.

"He—he—he—was supposed to *help* me," I wailed aloud.

I heard Frau Steiner's voice from the top of the stairs, "Ludolph Christoph Steiner, what on earth have you done to that poor boy? You'll wake the baby!"

I tried to swallow everything that was coming out—all the sorrow, all the fear, all the pent up grief, but it kept coming. It was a fountain that could not be shut off, a fountain of tears and low shuddering moans. The works of many writers I have read describe crying among men as a kind of dignified thing. A man will shed a single tear, if any at all. I know that now to be a lie, but at that point if I had believed that fallacy at all I would have labeled this as the crying of a small boy.

A small boy who has lost his only parent and was now well and truly alone in the world.

I felt a second hand on my back. Frau Steiner had come down the stairs and was now kneeling by me. She shushed me and stroked my hair, staring into my eyes with all the love and compassion of Mary, mother of God. Doktor Steiner retreated at the behest of his wife, who cradled me until the body wracking sobs finally slowed to a trickle. It seemed the fountain had run dry for now. My eyes hurt and my nose was a fountain of wet, flowing snot.

The doctor came back with a bottle and a wet rag. Frau Steiner wiped my face clean, staring into my eyes as though her gaze were an anchor holding me in the here and now. When my face was scoured red and I could feel the cold water evaporating on my skin the doctor pulled the cork from the bottle and offered me a swig.

I took it, wincing at the immediate sting of it in my mouth. That set me to coughing and choking in surprise. And the surprise distracted me from my sorrow. A pleasant warmth spread down my throat and suffused into the rest of my chest.

"Whiskey," he explained. "Cheap, but I do not drink it for recreation. Usually it is to help put a patient at ease when I must do something drastic. But the…lingering effects can also help calm a boy down when his grief threatens to overwhelm him.

"Now then," he squatted across from me, brushing a strand of my over-long hair from my eyes. "What happened?"

Over the next while I relayed my story. It took longer than I thought, and by the time I was finishing, the three of us were sitting over a supper of knockwurst with spoetzel and peas. I left out all of the parts about the monster, of course. In my mind I tried to rationalized him as some kind of exceedingly ugly bandit, and so that is how I painted him for the Steiners.

"He must have something against your father," the doctor said between mouthfuls of food. "But with your father dead, why does he pursue you still?"

I shook my head. I did not know. The thorn of my father's death still hurt, but it was no longer the fresh scraping wound that it had been in the Steiner's wing back chair. It was now a dull throb, a physical thing I could still feel catching my throat from time to time, but scarred over. Crying had helped, as had talking it out. Of course the large mug of beer that the doctor prescribed me over dinner also helped. It was thick and reminded me of fresh baked bread.

At the end of the night they apologized for not being able to help me find my father's friend and set me up with a cot beneath a window upstairs. The baby stayed with them in their room, though I could tell this open space was to belong to little Elisa when she was grown enough not to need to sleep with them at night.

Full of the heady feeling of beer, and tucked into warm blankets by Frau Steiner's hands I slipped into the first truly restful sleep I'd had in a very long time.

Chapter 5

Backdoor Hospitality

Restful though it was, there was not much to be had. I woke before the sun was up, even before the rest of the house had risen. No moonlight shone through the window above my head, though I knew it would be nearing full. I began to rise to look out the window when some primal sense in the back of my head screamed to lie still. I strained my ears and listen to the sounds of the house.

In the other room I could hear one of the Steiners snoring, and the quiet fussy sounds of the baby Elisa. From the floor below I could hear the thin regular ticking of a mantle clock echoing in the sitting room. What else did I hear? Something was missing.

I squeezed my eyes shut, realizing. There were no animal noises. Nothing from the mule or the horses. No song of May frogs. No crickets. It was, as they say, too quiet.

Something must have woken me, though. It was not the slow gentle waking of one's body rousing after a restful night. It was the abrupt and fully aware consciousness of someone made to wake. So what woke me? I strained my ears, almost knowing what I would hear before I heard it.

Something paced outside in the grass. It snuffled, and every great while grunted. The pulse froze in my neck as I heard that sound. And it was close. It had to be coming from the yard—it had to be below my window.

Its whinging, sly voice muttered, "I smell you, boy-child. Come outside so that these people do not become involved in our dispute."

A picture flash in my mind, unbidden. Elisa thrown in the well, Doktor and Frau Steiner dragged the half mile to the creek or pushed beneath the surface of a rain barrel. I lay, petrified. That subconscious voice in my mind warned me that if I moved it was all over.

"Give me what is mine," the river-thing cooed. "I was promised it."

I wanted to scream. I wanted to ask why it hunted me. I wanted to demand explanation. Instead, I couldn't even breath. I felt like a hand squeezed my throat. My lungs burned.

Couldn't I even pull my blankets over my head? I wanted to retreat into the safe fort of my covers like I had when I was six the night after Mother had told me the story of Hansel and Gretel. No, the voice screamed. No, if you move it is all over.

"I know you are in this house, first born. Come out now and it all ends. But if not…"

If not what? My muscles creaked, fighting the urge to sit up and look outside at my tormentor. Somewhere in the distance a cow lowed.

"If not then I can wait," it said with an air of final certainty.

I am not sure how I managed to fall asleep after the terror that gripped me like an iron band across the chest. Somehow I must have, though. I woke to a knock on the door and the sound of Doktor Steiner walking to it. Weak morning light was filling the space I slept in, turning the walls and the floor pale blue.

The terror was gone. I pushed myself upright with no restriction and climbed out of my cot. I crept to the edge of the stairs and peered down. There was a stressed murmur of conversation. Frau Steiner joined her husband at the door and the doctor sent a furtive glance up the stairs at me. I frowned, and I wondered. What was the problem?

"I will not," Steiner said more loudly. He seemed to be addressing more than just the men before him. "Do not do this, brethren. To do such would be wickedness."

Again Frau Steiner glanced at me, and I crept back from the stairs out of sight. The argument continued until finally Doktor Steiner shut the door on the men.

Frau Steiner spoke, just loud enough to hear. "You may come down, Herr Kirchner."

I came halfway down the stairs, gripping the banister as though it were a life-line. "What is the problem?"

The doctor was pacing around his examination table. "There have been animal mutilations in the night and a man's daughter has gone missing."

The iron band returned, and I could say nothing.

"The last time an outsider came to us, there was also death. He left before we could catch him, but there has been talk that the devil walks among us. The deaths stopped for awhile, but apparently have resumed."

I opened my mouth, but no words came. I stared at them. Doktor Steiner stared up at me from beside his table and the Frau bounced baby Elisa on her hip. Finally my voice returned.

“It was not me. I was—I was in the house the whole night!”

He nodded. “I believe you. And I would not give you over to those men. Our town is fearful, and might do something to damn their souls in that fear.”

“What do I do, then?” I asked.

He moved out of the examination room and into the kitchen. I came down the stairs following him, and Frau Steiner came behind us.

“You must leave now,” he said. He pulled a potato sack from beside the cabinet and began filling it with dry goods from inside—apples, breads, anything he could lay his hands on. “This will see you for a while. I will distract the men and tell them that I am sending Edda to fetch you. While they are distracted you must leave out the back and take your mule.”

He shoved the sack into my hands. “Go, now!”

I took the bag and my things and he moved back to the front of the house. When he opened the door again I could hear him relaying the lie to his townsmen. That was when Frau Steiner opened the door and I escaped into the yard.

The pen given over to the horses pulled me short in my steps. The horses remained, but they threw their heads frightfully and cowered in one corner of the pen. Foam gathered at their lips. There, on the opposite end was a bloody patch in the grass. My mule was gone.

My mule was gone.

The feeling struck like a hammer to my chest. I froze, indecisive. It was only Frau Steiner’s voice at the back door whispering, “Go! Go!” that set me back in motion.

I ran the first few miles. I jogged a few more after that. Exhaustion dragged me to a walk beyond that. And it was that tired walk that carried me into Muscatine late that evening, saddlebags sloped over one shoulder and the Sharps and potato stack turned into a makeshift bindle.

The saloons were open and active with crews off the paddleboats but otherwise the streets were quiet. Muscatine was not a raucous town, just a busy one. I could not help but stare into the windows of houses as I passed. There I saw families lit in the warm glow of candles and oil lamps gathered close and enjoying each other's company. Mothers darned socks or mended clothes while fathers puffed on pipes and read to the children. I found myself yearning to hear what stories were told in those houses, and my feet nearly carried me to a few windows in particular.

It was as I was passing the dry goods shop that I heard a voice call out to me.

"Boy, yeah you there. Boy!"

I turned. The shopkeeper was standing by the door of his shop, key slotted in the lock. He looked at my load and smiled.

"You ever find your friend?"

I shook my head.

"Thought not. Did some thinking and asked a pal or two of mine. Partner of mine works the dock said he had a Henry Clay take passage just to get 'cross the water into Illinois. Guess he was headed toward Springfield."

I nodded slowly and thanked him.

"You look like you got drug halfway here from Amana. You alright boy?"

"Just tired." I didn't even bother to hide my accent.

He rubbed his chin a moment. "Tell you what. You want, I got some spare floor space in my attic back at the house. Git you a blanket and you can use a bag of flour for a pillow. T'aint much, but it's out of the weather." He sniffed. "Smells like it's gonna rain, too."

Sleep was troubled that night. I was far from any windows, but every so often I thought I heard a voice on the other side of the walls whisper, "Soon…soon…"

In Springfield I asked after Samuel Henry Clayton, Sam Clayton, Henry Clay, Samuel Clay, and even Henry Samuel Clay on a whim. The latter garnered the attention of a wild-eyed drunk. Against my better judgment I followed the man into the alleyway between a fur trading company and a shipping company's office.

The drunk eyed me with suspicion, as though he were leery of having followed a strange boy into an alleyway where the boy might club him and take his bottle. I tolerated the looks and the potency of his breath.

He spoke first, leaning over me. "What you know about Henry Samuel Clay?"

I shrugged uncomfortably, backing up to the brick wall. "N-nothing. I was told to look for him."

"By *whom*?" he asked with ridiculous emphasis.

I shook my head. "My father."

"Why your pappy want him?"

I took a deep breath, screwing up my courage. "Can you tell me where he is or not?"

"Gotta know I can trust you." He took a swig of the whiskey and wiped the lip with his sleeve. "Want some?"

“Egh, no thank you.” I tried to give a grateful smile, but I do not believe I succeeded. “My father said he could help me.”

“And where is he now, eh?”

I looked at the dirt at our feet. “He’s—he’s dead.”

The drunk sobered up. I could feel him watching me, though I continued to stare into the dirt. I didn’t want to look on his face. I’d seen so much pity already. Pity is the most useless of all emotions, and I refused to see that look in someone’s face again.

He cleared his throat. “Well—ehm—it was somethin’ unnatural warn’t it?”

I nodded, still focusing on his toes. I would not cry, not again.

“He helped me like that, too. Some creature stumbling out of this rail car bound for Chicago from out Egypt-ways. All bandaged like. Killed three of my friends afore I got out of the boat. I would’a made four if Henry Samuel Clay ain’t come along when he did. He killed it. For good. Told me never to tell nobody.”

I looked up. His face was gray and drawn. I suddenly had a small inkling of why he’d crawled into the bottle. I couldn’t fathom seeing that with my own eyes and not doing the same.

“Why did you tell me?” I asked with a small croaking voice.

“Telling makes it better. I figure you know what’s what. A man can’t see that and not tell someone. It kills you. Slower’n a bullet, but just as surely.”

I nodded. “I think I understand.”

The drunk sagged and pulled away from me. "Your pappy wanted you to find Henry Samuel Clay? He gone north. Told it was some logging camp along the St. Croix. There was murders in the newspaper up there what interested him."

"Thank you," I said and turned to leave.

He grabbed the sleeve of my coat. "Hey."

I stopped.

"Was your thing all bandaged up too?"

I shook my head. "No. Mine was something else."

"What was it?"

"I don't know. I was hoping Mr. Clayton would know."

His hand dropped from my sleeve, and he looked like he might cry. I began to leave again and stopped, looking over my shoulder. He stared at his bottle, despondent.

Clearing my throat, I said, "It is Sunday and I have not seen a church in some time. Would you—would you come with me?"

The drunk stared at me for a moment. Clouds parted in his gaze and he gave me a brief smile.

Chapter 6

A Town With No Name

I crossed the river with the first ferry run of the morning. The men at the rope were still bleary eyed, nipping at bottles or flasks to stave off thunderous hangovers. It was just early enough that mist like the ghosts of clouds hung above the waters of the St. Croix.

Each swirl and eddy of water caused my heart to stumble and skip a beat. I kept expecting a hand to unfurl out of the cold river water and grasp the boat, dragging us down. I was certain somewhere out there I would see the bulbous, sickly looking eyes of the creature poking up from the water. I certainly felt its oily gaze. Though for my sake and the sake of the ferry men and other passengers, it seemed the river-thing would not show itself.

The logging camp squatted on the opposite bank, a broad collection of squat buildings. All the wood was new, still golden or yellow cut and more roofs were canvas than not. To the north of the camp was a broad expanse of land cleared of timber, running miles up and past the river's bend. The trees were chopped and then loaded into the river to float down to the camp's mill. The south end of the camp was still thick wilderness.

Weeks of inquiring at every community I crossed north finally led me here, to this little speck on the map of the American frontier. This place without a name, belonging to the Harolds & Farthing Lumber Company, Chicago, est. 1851.

The wood beneath my feet thumped as the boat smacked into land. The ferry men tied down the boats while I and the other passengers climbed off. I was shoved aside by men twice my size and age as they shouldered their way into the camp. I stopped to gawk at the mess of the camp and caught a cuff across the back of my head from a man trying to make his way past me.

Oh, certainly the camp had the makings of a town. There was a canvas-walled saloon, a tarpaulin roofed church (small as it was), and a collection of tents circled by board planks stomped into the mud that served as a house of ill repute (and a laundry and bath house, besides). These were the first whores I'd seen in my life, and I think I must have stared at them the most. But everything felt too temporary, ephemeral, to ever become a real town.

A pair of ladies airing blankets outside the bordello saw my gawping and laughed. Each was of the roughest cut of woman that the frontier produced in those days. Filthy, bedraggled, clothed only in their white-ish underthings. They gossiped and traded bawdy jokes as I began to walk past them.

"A mite young to be wandering around these parts, ain't ya?" one of the women asked.

Her—ah—*décolletage* was on display, even at this time of morning and I could hardly look in her direction much less eye contact for worry that I'd leer. I kept my eyes to the mud road which sucked at my boots rather than make eye contact.

"I'm, uh, just looking for someone." I hastily added a respectful, "Ma'am," onto the end.

“Lookin’ for your pappy?” the other one asked. They came out into the road, bare feet heedless of the awful slush of the road. “Lots of them around these parts.”

That set them to giggling, though the joke was above my head. The excuse was a good one, though—or so I thought.

“Ah, yes. I am looking for my father.”

The first one smiled, squatting down beside me to look up at me. She wore no makeup, and was surrounded by filth and squalor but you would have never known it looking at her. She was confident and regal, a queen in stained linens. She extended a hand to me, fingers long and nimble.

“My name is Ginny Catskill. What’s yours?”

“Charlie Ki—ah—Charlie Clayton.” I just prayed he was using that last name here.

The way she smiled carried all the morning warmth the air was missing. “You don’t sound like a Clayton.”

I cleared my throat, my cheeks burning. “My mother. My mother was German.”

“Was?”

I bit my lip.

“Dearie, no wonder you’re looking for your pappy. What’s his name?”

“Samuel Henry Clayton. He might go by Henry Clay.”

She blanched at the name, and I wondered if something bad had happened here already.

“Lots o’ names, huh? We know lots o’ boys around here with lots o’ names, don’t we Laurel?”

Laurel nodded grimly by Ginny’s side. “We surely do, Virginia. Mighty lots of men come and hide out in Nowhere when they’ve been in a few too many gun fights.”

It made sense, I supposed. If you were a wanted man, or you were a bit too loose with a gun, I could see the sense in taking on a different name. Still, I frowned. Ginny, always studying my face, placed her hands firmly on my shoulders and squeezed.

"Don't you worry, darling boy, I'm sure as anything your pappy is a fine and upstanding man. It's just, you know what they say: two names is surely heavy when you're traveling fast. Guessing you don't have a place to stay?"

I shook my head.

"And no money to boot," she supposed.

"I spent the last penny on the ferry."

She smiled sadly. "Well Charlie, I can help. I'll call in a favor and have you tented up with someone. Sound good?"

I stammered, my face burning. "No, no. I couldn't, that would—I do not want to impose."

Ginny and Laurel fell into gales of laughter.

"Oh, Virginia darlin' I think he thinks we're offering to let him stay with us."

Ginny wiped tears from her eyes and gave me a swift hug, pecking me on the cheek. "Dear boy, no offense but live-in-men is bad for business, and children too. You're of an age to be either. I'll find a good safe place for you, though. Well and away from them desperados what work the saws and axes. Come on, let's find you a warm place to incubate your crumbs."

"My what?"

"To sleep. You'll want it if you don't find your pappy a'fore night."

She stood, folding my hand into hers and as boyish as it sounds I'll tell you right now: Virginia Catskill was the first woman I ever fell in love with.

Chapter 7

Samuel Henry Clayton

In all the chaos there was a kind of order in the logging camp. It was not an order enforced by foremen, or even the fat man in the fine suit who walked the camp with his fine cigar and fine hat barking fine orders. It was a natural order, the way the chaos of your guts and organs and body turns into the rhythm of your heart and the pulse of your life. Men rose, men ate, men worked.

The work was just beginning as Miss Ginny walked me away from the brothel. The man in charge was evidently also the man running the saloon. "Blue Beaver" was painted in blue letters crudely above the canvas flap he pushed his way out of. He came to berate her for leaving her station.

"House, you know damn well not a single man appears a'fore afternoon. Mind yours and I'll mind mine."

"Minding yours *is* minding mine, Ginny! You're the most popular saddle. I need you back and waiting for customers."

She cuffed him once over the head and pointed at me. "This poor boy is wandering all by his lonesome in need of his father. If I can't help him find his pappy, the least I can do is make sure he gets a place to sleep where he won't be robbed blind by the first log chewer what finds him."

The blow took most of the fight out of him. The words took care of the rest. He gave me one baleful glare and slunk back to his saloon.

Miss Ginny took me around, curling a strand of her hair in her fingers any time she saw a place she thought she might stow me. Then she'd shake her head and say something like, "No, he'll cheat you," or, "He got no place to put you."

Midway through she brought me to a small awning in front of a log building that looked to be the logging camp's office. A line of men, many of which I recognized from the ferry across the river, stared openly at Ginny as we walked past them. She guided me right to the front of the line, giving a smile and a wink to any men who protested. A man with a log book eyed the Sharps on my shoulder and my saddlebags under my arm as we came up.

"Looks a little young for a log chewer," he said.

Ginny planted a hand on my shoulder. "Charlie here is looking for his daddy. What's his name, Charlie?"

"Samuel Clayton?"

"Know when he came in?" the man asked.

"Some time in the last few weeks."

He scanned his books. "No Samuel Clayton."

"What about Samuel or Henry Clay? Something like that?"

He looked again and shook his head. "No, sorry son."

We walked away, Ginny frowning. "You're sure it was this camp, Charlie?"

I nodded. "Yes."

Ginny idly tugged at a girl of hair. "Well if nothing else, we'll keep looking for a place for you to stay in the meantime."

At last we came to a boathouse hanging out over the water. The sight of it made me swallow. "Bill Aberdeen should have a place for you," she said. "You can rest your head on a buoy or something."

"I'd rather not," I confessed.

She turned a skeptical frown on me. "Well why ever not?"

I cleared my throat, grasping for an excuse. "I'm…I can't swim."

"Nonsense. I'm not askin' you to sleep in the water. Now come on." And she hauled me up and into that boathouse. It stood on a little rise overlooking the water, jutting out over it. I wasn't sure I couldn't feel the river-thing's eyes on me as I walked into that shack that smelled like dust and fish.

Inside Bill Aberdeen was hammering away at an old flat bottom roped up above a great hole in the floor that looked over the river. The far end of the room was dedicated to a huge pair of doors that would open to let the boat out onto the river. They were open at this time, and you could hear the first axes of the morning echoing off the distant woods like the sound of staccato coughing.

Mister Aberdeen drew to his feet as Miss Ginny and I walked in, pulling his hat off his head and clutching it to his chest like a bouquet of flowers.

"Why, Ginny! To what do I owe the singular pleasure?"

"I need a place for my friend here to bed down tonight. Mind letting him stay in here?"

He eyed me suspiciously. "He one o' yours?"

Miss Ginny cuffed him over the ear like she'd cuffed the pimp. "Do I *look* old enough to have whelped this young man?"

"Ow! Ow!" He danced around, rubbing at the struck head. After that it didn't take much more argument for him to agree.

Ginny pointed to a far corner. "You can put your things in here, sugar."

Mister Aberdeen eyed me and I eyed him back. He didn't want me to sleep here and I didn't much want to do the sleeping. Still, he didn't protest. I propped the rifle along a cabinet full of bottles and fishing tackle and laid my saddlebags and the potato sack next to it.

When Miss Ginny and I parted ways I began my search. As they day drew to its full height the camp filled with noise. Saws sawing, axes chopping, and the mill running a loud whine. Naturally my search took me as far from the river as possible. I made plans to come back to the boathouse that night for my things and just hide in the woods if I could find any place sufficiently far from water.

I asked high and low, ranging the cleared miles around the mill and into the woods. Most men didn't know who I was talking about, but every now and then I would find a lead that would take me further into the forest.

"I think I know the man," a lumberjack would say. "Saw him poking around the potter's field.

Another told me, "I could swear I saw a man looked like a gunslinger stalking about the logging sites."

A gnarled man hanging by a belt from a tree confided to me in shouts, "That's the man what's here for the bounty on the Hidebehind, yeah?"

"What's a Hidebehind?" I asked.

A lumberjack nearby made the sign of the cross and another laughed. "Don't listen to him. Folk are saying there's a monster hides in the woods killing loggers. This is dangerous work. People die every day. Ain't nothing more than that."

"They call it a Hidebehind 'cause it can hide behind any tree," the religious logger said. "And it *is* killing. Ain't no normal mortality."

Several times men chased me away as they worked, swatting at me with hats or berating me. As evening set on, the leads began taking me back into the camp. A full day was passed with no success. I made note of a few likely places to camp and began my trek to gather my things.

"Little Charlie!" a couple of the girls called as I passed the whores' tents. One, Miss Ginny's friend Laurel came up into the street with another girl and gave me a quick hug. "Find your pappy?"

"Nothing yet. Have you seen Ginny? I wanted to thank her for her help."

"She's…with a customer. Buck up Charlie." She graced me with a peck on the cheek and again I had to hide my eyes to keep from blushing at the sight of her. "I heard something you might like."

"What is that?"

The other girl tittered, hiding a smile behind her hand. "Why he's as red as an apple!"

"Shush, Edith. Charlie, honey, I hear your pappy wanders 'round the camp asking odd questions. He's usually in the saloon at night though." Behind her were the enthusiastic sounds of a few women and their customers. I was sure my ears burned red. Mentally I recited *Our Father…*

I nearly asked what he looked like, but realized that would be a silly question for a son to ask. Instead, I thanked her and walked through the mud to the Blue Beaver. The place hummed with noise and the tarpaulin roof glowed with lamps being lit as the sun began to disappear behind the trees. I crossed the canvas flap into the mouth of the saloon and steeled myself.

I'm not sure what I expected. Perhaps I was half expecting Mister Clayton to be the only man there, sitting by his lonesome. He'd look up at me, nod, and invite me to have a drink and talk business. In reality what I found was a room slowly filling up with filthy, exhausted workers, bare chested or in their shirt sleeves, all working off the day's stress with mugs of beer or glasses of liquor.

I began to wander, drawing curious looks from some of the camp workers. I stopped one man and made the standard inquiries and he pointed to the saw-horse bar. I knew the man he was pointing to straight away. Where every other man at the bar talked and laughed and drank with the others one figure stood apart.

Perhaps it was his clothing. Every lumberjack and log runner was stripped to their shirtsleeves while he still wore a frock coat and wide brimmed grey hat. Perhaps it was the way he held himself. There was an aura of exhaustion in the crowd that did not touch him, and there was a cloud of suspicion and coolness that gathered around him like a cloak against sociability.

Samuel Henry Clayton. At last.

I sucked in a breath and gathered my courage. I crossed the floorboards to him and cleared my throat. "Excuse me sir. I need your help."

A man like a side of beef shoved past me to lay hand on Mister Clayton's shoulder. Mister Clayton turned with the hand regarding it and then the man attached to it with no great care. He brushed the hand aside.

"Can I help you?" He ignored me in favor of the Chuck Roast who addressed him. A calm hand swept one side of the frock coat aside revealing a pistol.

Chuck Roast glanced at it. Blued steel contrasted against a tarnished brass frame glittering in the smoky lamplight. He picked at the lapel of Samuel Clayton's jacket and said, "I seen you walking around here a lot, Johnny Reb. You a company man?"

"Mayhaps I am."

"You don't look like no company man, Johnny Reb."

Mister Clayton's eyes slid from one side of Chuck Roast's head to the other. The conversation hadn't dimmed, but quietly men were beginning to stand. "S'pose you're going to tell me what I look like."

"You look like a freeloader and a damned traitor. You around here, sniffing up our asses and wandering our woods. Then you come back here and prig our women and drink our liquor. Me? I think you're here scoutin' for your guerrilla friend thinking to take our payroll."

The room now fell quiet. Mister Clayton rolled his eyes. He had a square and stern face off-set with a full but cropped beard. His whole appearance seemed custom built for sardonic expressions and deadpan glares. He held up two fingers.

"Two points." Mister Clayton ticked off the first finger. "First: I ain't had, nor had time for, any of your women."

He ticked off the second finger. “Second: ain’t your booze ‘til you pay for it.”

That caused Chuck Roast to think, as much as it seemed to pain him. Whatever occurred in his head, he didn’t like it. The next moment he grabbed Clayton’s lapel and tried to yank him into his fist.

I never saw the moment he drew his gun. What I saw was the gun seem to materialize with the muzzle pressing into the fleshy part of Chuck Roast’s neck where it met the jaw.

Chuck Roast withdrew his fists and stepped back. Mister Clayton kept his gun trained on the lumberjack while one hand wandered to his glass of whiskey. The whole room watched as he lifted it to his lips and downed it in one go.

“Take my glass,” he said.

Chuck Roast came in close and froze at the ratcheting sound of Samuel cocking the pistol.

Samuel’s face was grim. “Easy, Yankee.”

When Chuck Roast took the glass Mister Clayton began to back away toward the canvas flap, offering the business end of his shooting iron to anyone who flinched in his direction. Clayton’s step was only slightly slurred by drink.

Chuck Roast growled and said, “This ain’t over, Johnny Reb.”

“It’s over for now.”

And that’s when the first fist swung, from an unseen lumberjack, almost catching him off guard.

I just managed to squeak out the entrance, ahead of the brawl that erupted. I waited anxiously outside for any sign of Samuel Clayton, wringing my hands. To my surprise I heard not one gunshot though through the bubbled, cheap windows I could see it had boiled into every man for himself.

A figure black against the lamplight stumbled out of the Blue Beaver. He straightened his jacket and donned his hat before walking on. A moment afterward company enforcers thundered through the mud and into the saloon. The discharge of pistols cracked the summer night like lightning and I saw fresh holes punch through the canvas roof. The cacophony of the brawl quieted immediately.

I stole through the night then, and followed Samuel Clayton. He walked past the brothel where women were coming out into the street watching the Beaver, and past several out buildings belonging to the logging company. He traveled past the camps, and then maybe a quarter mile out into the wild. All the while he muttered and cursed to himself. He had seemed sober enough in the Blue Beaver, but several times I saw him pull a flask from his pocket and nip at it.

A camp was laid out in a hollow in the ground and a horse was tethered there, cropping at grass. I waited in the dark while he roamed ahead of me and began arranging wood and tinder. A few sparks stood out in the night and soon a red and orange glow blossomed, illuminating his face. It was him.

"Samuel Henry Clayton?" I asked, stepping into the ring of light.

The pistol was in his hand and half out of the holster by the time he saw me. He relaxed a little, but not much. It was like watching a cougar pacing, sizing up its prey.

"You were in the saloon," he said.

I nodded and tried to calm myself. The moment of truth. "Mister Clayton, I was told you can help me."

His face was suspicious, appraising. To my surprise the only stain on his face after the fight was a bruise left by that first punch. Otherwise he appeared untouched.

"That depends on the kind of help." He withdrew the Remington fully and laid it in his lap. I came closer and he held up a hand, stopping me short.

"What's your name, son?"

"Charlie. Charles Florian Kirchner. I think you knew my father."

He did not relax exactly. More, he sagged. Samuel looked down at his pistol regretfully, a thumb spinning the cylinder.

"It finally came for him, didn't it?"

When I said nothing Samuel hung his head and took a long sigh. "Failed him," I thought I heard him say. When he looked up again the flickering fire light made his face look haggard and tired. He reached into the inside pocket of his coat and took a nip from a leather sleeved flask.

I swallowed. "Your friend Samson said you can help with things that are—eh—beyond the pale."

His face was shadowed by the firelight. "Son, the trouble you're in is far west of pale. Do you know what was hunting your father?"

I shook my head.

He sighed, pulling off his hat to run a hand through his shaggy brown hair. "Look, I have a job here that needs tending."

I began to protest. "But what about-"

“There are people dying here. Sometimes four in a week. I. Need. To. Stay. Here.” He stabbed the dirt with a finger to emphasize each word.

“It’s hunting me now, though. What do I do?”

Clayton rose and began pacing, picking up twigs to snap them and toss them in the fire. He was silent for a real long time and I began to wonder if he would send me back home, back to my death. I wondered for the thousandth time if I would be left to die a strangled death in a river. I think I must have made a whimpering sound as he turned to look at me finally, thinking out loud.

“Stay close. Nearby. I can come if you need help. Took him decades to find your old man, could take him longer to find you.”

I shivered and looked over my shoulder into the dark.

“It’s—he’s followed me here, I think.”

“Where you staying?”

“I have a corner in the boathouse—”

“Foolish,” he muttered.

“But I was hoping to get my things and find a better camp. I—I don’t want to be that close to the water.”

“Good.” Clayton turned to where his things were stowed and pulled out a Dance revolver and a Henry rifle. “You good with either of these?”

I tried to give a nonchalant shrug, but the Henry held my rapt attention. The Dance & Brothers revolver was a cheap Confederate knockoff of the superior Patterson Colt six-guns, but the Henry rifle…I had heard legends of these mechanical wonders—swift firing and accurate. In the hands of even a modest sharp shooter you could rain down a veritable fire storm.

"I have a Sharps that belonged to my father back in the boathouse."

He frowned, mulling it over. He thrust the Henry into my hands and I tried not to look giddy. Some things do not change, and one thing I've noticed is that even today all boys (and some girls) are fascinated by guns.

Mister Clayton mimicked holding the rifle, working the lever. "This is easier to load than the six-shooter. Pull the lever to load the next round after firing." He mimed the motion. I nodded and practiced the motion with the rifle. When he was satisfied he fished some cartridges from his pocket and saddlebags and handed them to me. After showing me how to load the rifle he pulled a massive single-edged knife out of his belt sheath and passed it to me grip-first.

"Backup. Thing gets too close don't even bother with the rifle. Drop it and use this."

I nodded and took the knife. I felt dizzy even at the thought of the river-thing getting so close.

"Good. Let's go get your things."

Chapter 8

The Boathouse

Much of everything was dark. There were still campfires in the tents, live and tended. Lights burned in the Blue Beaver but no conversation came out of it. As we passed Ginny's little commune the foreman of the camp was dragging men out and into the street, shouting at them to get some goddamned sleep. So it made sense that the boathouse was dark when we returned.

There were no locks on the door when we climbed the stoop. Mister Clayton brushed past me, insisting on being the first one in. The hammer of his pistol clicked as he drew it back, and then he gently opened the door.

Upon his instruction I waited until he had lit a lantern and inspected the place. When he finally muttered "Clear," I came in after. The large doors at the other end of the house were closed up for the night.

Mister Clayton struck a match and lit a lantern on the shelf, casting the room in a smoked yellow. His hard eyes searched around, and I saw that they were starting to be bloodshot now. Still, the room seemed to be clear. I breathed a sigh of relief and went to the corner with my things.

It must have come when Mister Clayton was not looking. We heard nothing as it slipped from the water. I was checking my things for signs of theft and Mister Clayton was prodding through cabinets for danger.

I knew nothing of its presence until it grabbed both my arms. I yelped in surprise as I was pulled toward the water.

The enclosed space filled painfully with the pop of gunfire. One bullet buzzed past our heads like a hornet and the next struck true. I heard it hit home behind me and the river-thing released me.

I spun on it, fumbling for the Henry set aside while I was gathering my things. I saw it, saw the river-thing in the light for the first time.

It clutched at the side of its head, mouth wide and hissing death at us. It had man's face, but green—eyes slightly too large, slightly too far apart and a toothless mouth that split its face like a gash.

Green ooze like pond scum leaked from between its webbed, clawed fingers clutched at the bullet hole in the side of its head. It opened its mouth, swollen tongue lolling.

Samuel shouted "Charlie, look out!"

The tongue struck me in the face and knocked me against the wall. Lights flashed in my vision. My face was enveloped, my ears too—sight and sound strangled. What I know is that I was yanked off my feet and by the sudden pull to the creature. Damp arms clutched me across my neck and chest and the tongue ripped painfully from my face. The room spun, and I still reeled from the blow.

"Shoot me and you shoot him," the river-thing croaked in German.

Mister Clayton shot him.

The tongue retracted and I felt like my head was coming out of water. The thing pulled away from me, hissing again. It took two fumbling, bleeding steps and fell into the water in the center of the boathouse.

Mister Clayton fired three more shots into the water after it. He stuffed the Remington back into its holster and pulled the Dance revolver from where it was pinned in his belt.

"Get your things," he shouted with the pistol trained on the water. "We're leaving, now."

"You speak Deutsch?" I asked, stunned.

Samuel paused, looking at me askance. "What?"

"You knew what it said when it threatened me."

He snorted. "I got the gist."

Perhaps it was just residue left on my face by the thing's tongue, but the whole place smelled of water rot to me. I looked behind me to see a splash of more of that awful sticky green blood on the wall. The daze of the attack faded as I gathered my things from the corner, but I could feel my shoulders starting to bruise.

When we burst out of the boathouse the camp was alive again. Samuel slung the potato sack over his shoulder and ran low with the Dance revolver in the other hand. Lights appeared in all the tents and most of the company and auxiliary buildings and down the river bank the worker tents buzzed with activity.

"They heard the gunshots," Mister Clayton said. He didn't elaborate further, but I got the message: they'd be looking for a murder.

To my surprise though, no one came toward the boathouse. No one approached us. The bordello girls were all standing outside the tents clutching nightgowns or corsets close and staring into the black. I recognized Laurel and Edith among them. Several times we saw clusters of men, but each time they were gathering together with torches and guns and running out and into the woods.

As we ran Mister Clayton's gaze became more searching and his frown deepened. Finally our pace slowed and I spoke up.

"They're not hunting us, are they?"

He shook his head.

"It's whatever you're here for, isn't it?"

He nodded.

"And you need to go?"

Mister Clayton turned, handing me the potato sack and taking the Henry from me. "I'm finding out what's what. You're finding some place with people. Buy a poke if you have to."

"A poke?"

"Stay with the whores."

I gawped. "Mister Clayton, I don't—"

"No time for scandalizing. There's killing out there." He shoved me back. "Go on, get!"

Before I could further protest he was running off. I stood in the middle of that muddy roadway looking this way and that. My shoulders ached where the river-thing had pulled me, and my face felt crusty and sticky with slime. If someone were to ask me, I'd tell them that there was nowhere I felt safe except with Mister Clayton. He had already proved the magic ingredient for protecting me. That made up my mind.

I ran after him, catching up with him as he was pushing his way through a kicked anthill of angry workers. Men shouted, demanding to know what was going on or threatening to leave if no one answered. The man with the very fine suit was trying to address them.

"I assure you, we are doing our square best to hunt this animal down," he said with arms held high.

"The Hidebehind done kilt twelve men in the last month!" someone shouted. A chorus of scared agreement rippled out from him.

"And two more tonight!" Again the rippling chorus.

The company man was not dissuaded. "This is not some mythical monster, gentlemen. It's just an animal, and it can be killed. There is a cash bounty of fifty dollars to the man who brings us the pelt of the creature. You can bring it to the office and I will personally sign the check."

"Gold don't do us no good if we're kilt!"

I grabbed Mister Clayton's coat sleeve. He turned and glared down at me.

"I told you to get to safety."

I thrust out my chin stubbornly. "I am."

"You want none of this business. Go on now. Get."

"You proved to me back there that you are the safest place I can be."

He glared at me for a moment. He studied me, short and skinny as I was. The weeks of travel had burned away the last of my baby fat and left me lean and wiry. He eyed the rifle.

"You really, truly know how to use that?"

I nodded.

"No dying," he said and turned his back on me.

The company man stood beside, shivering, with a vacant look in his eyes. Someone had thrust a tin cup of coffee into the foreman's hand but he made no motion to drink from it. Samuel listened to the prattling scared questions of the camp workers and the just-as-scared and just-as-prattling answers of the company man. While he listened he pulled a battered silver case from inside his jacket and withdrew a thin brown cigarillo from it. Chomped between his teeth he pulled a match from another pocket and lit it on the heel of his boot.

I stepped beside him and watched as orange light underlit his face. The smell of liquor was strong enough on him that I wondered that he didn't catch alight and become a human blaze. After a few encouraging puffs on the cigarillo he pulled it from his teeth and inspected it. Finally he cleared his throat and asked his own question.

"And you're certain it was an animal?"

The crowd fell quiet. No few of them remembered his face from the Blue Beaver. The company man mopped sweat from his brow. Not nervous sweat, just sweat. It was a hot evening.

The company man bristled. "Are you suggesting you believe in fairy tales?"

"I ain't suggesting anything. And I ain't asking *you*." Mister Clayton waved his cigarillo at the foreman. "You there."

The foreman stirred for the first time and met Mister Clayton's gaze. He looked down at the cup in his hands, startled to see it. The night fell silent but for the persistent trilling of summer frogs.

"It was a cat—leasting I think it were," he said. His voice poured out as a melodious Irish brogue. "I saw it take McClellan. Dragged him into the woods, it did."

Mister Clayton took another swig of his flask and replaced the cigar in his teeth. "Sure it weren't a dog? Big one, yea high?"

"No sir."

"What kind of cat?"

"Big one."

"Like a puma?"

The foreman thought for a moment and shook his head. "No—bigger."

"How big."

"Size of a Conestoga."

Some in the crowd actually laughed at the man's words. To them clearly the man was just shaken by his experiences. I remembered, though: the world only appeared to be rational.

The foreman protested. "It was the Hidebehind, I promise you. I was drinking, and it were that which saved me."

"Drinking?" I asked Mister Clayton softly but he waved a hand for me to quiet down.

The man's ridiculous claim stole the tension and anger from the crowd and they began to disperse. When the fringes of the crowd began to dissolve the company man shouted for men to return to their tents as if the dispersal were his own idea. Soon it was just the company man, the foreman, and us.

The company man wagged a finger at Mister Clayton. "Now hear this. You've been skulking around our camp for a long time. If you're not planning on taking a job, then I will have to ask you to leave. This land is property of—"

"I am here for a job," Mister Clayton said.

The company man hesitated, sensing his *but*.

"I'm here hunting your Hidebehind."

The other man drew up, indignant. “Superstition. And you’re taking this little boy along on your gallivanting across the countryside?”

Mister Clayton spat. His words were beginning to slur with drink. “This is my son.”

The man stared between the two of us. Mister Clayton with his long face and curly dark hair, and I with my straight Germanic nose and round features.

“Surely you’re joking. You two look nothing—”

Mister Clayton stared at the man until he stopped talking.

“Where was McClellan killed?”

The foreman pointed. “Field ‘round back of the survey office. We was closing up for the night when it came out’a nowhere.”

Mister Clayton tipped his hat and turned, heading back up the way toward the company buildings.

Chapter 9

Two Points

"Aw, shit." Mister Clayton realized his mistake about a tick too late. We came over the rise to find the end of the mile long trail. McClellan, or what remained of him, lay against a tree stump.

The mistake was allowing me to see McClellan. White flesh opened in black rents and yellow bone protruded from limbs. My vision swam, and I turned to retch.

"God's sake, boy. Don't foul up the site. I need to look for tracks."

"I can't help it!" I moaned, nauseous and only momentarily distracted from the sight of the body by the hurt inflicted upon me by his tone.

As we'd walked out there tracking the streaks of blood and scrapes of McClellan's feet, Mister Clayton had fallen more dour and sullen. Even now he continued to nip at the flask. He did not seem drunk per se, but he was not sober.

I wiped my mouth on my sleeve. Every time I closed my eyes I saw the chewed, mangled flesh. His face was intact and stared up at the clear night sky with a vague look of surprise. As if to say, "I had no idea there could be so many stars."

Mister Clayton squatted above the body, poking through it with one hand while holding the lantern high with the other. "See any tracks?"

"No?" I looked over my shoulder at him.

"Damnit, what good are you?"

I tried to protest, but gave it up. Instead I tromped around in the dark looking for tracks. Of what kind, I had no idea. I'd not know them if I saw them, but I wasn't sure I'd even find any. There had been no sign of the trail except what McClellan had left in his struggles and death.

"I don't think there are any tracks."

"Don't be silly. There has to be."

"But we've looked everywhere. I haven't found any, and I don't think you have either."

"Of course not. I've been looking over the body."

I dared not look in his direction. Even the mention of the body caused a roll in my gut. Instead I gazed out over the line of trees. We were near the place where open field chewed inexorably away at the woods, the place the loggers had not quite conquered yet. At this time of night, and blinded as I was by the lantern, I could still pick apart the woods from the black of the night. Above us the whole of the heavens made manifest its glory while the woods bore only the black of India ink.

Out of the corner of my eye I saw Samuel pick something up, sniff it, and blanch. I turned a little. It was a whiskey bottle.

"Weren't a Hidebehind."

"How do you know?"

"This man was drinking."

I turned fully to watch him. Thankfully his own form eclipsed most of the body. "Why do they avoid drunk men?"

Samuel shrugged. "Just always have. Don't have to make sense."

I disagreed to myself. Every creature had a reason for acting as it did—even Mister Clayton.

I turned away when he shifted, revealing the body again. I had to swallow hard to force down the rising tide of bile. After counting to ten to calm myself I began to search for tracks again.

A twinkling of lights caught my eyes, and I looked to the woods. I glanced at Mister Clayton and looked back. It was still there, but I couldn't quite make out what it was. I stepped away from the range of the lantern's light and tried to let my eyes adjust.

Mister Clayton spoke up. "You see something, boy?"

I clenched my eyes and once more counted to ten. When I opened them I could see the dark better. I could make out the shapes of the nearest trees now, and of the underbrush at their roots. And there, I saw it. Two faint pinpricks of light. Eyes in the night.

Watching us.

"Mister Clayton! There!" I pointed at the eyes.

He stumbled to his feet, nearly tripping over the ex-McClellan and grabbed his rifle. "Good eyes, boy. Stay here."

Mister Clayton darted as best he could toward the woods. The eyes disappeared and there was a sense of something moving, turning.

"It's running!" I shouted. Mister Clayton ran harder and vanished into the brush. The only sign of his passing was a quickly receding bob of yellow light.

Stay here.

I blinked. "Wait. He left me in the dark!" I bolted after him.

A gun fired deep in the woods and I ran toward that noise. But here is the problem with running in the woods, regardless of the time of day. Man was created for civilization. It is our natural habitat, the place where we are attuned to move most freely. The wild beast knows the woods, knows its ways. It is created and adapted to the woods and can slip through it as fast as a bolt and as silent as a prayer.

I was perhaps half a span into the trees when my foot caught a root. I tumbled end over end, stopped only by the trunk of a tree smacking my spine. Pain lanced through my body and I cried out. I tried to find my Sharps, dropped in the fall, but my hands landed in thorns.

By the time I was able to collect myself there were more gunshots to gauge my direction by. But I was more cautious now. I moved slowly, making sure of each step and casting my free hand out wide to catch anything before it caught me.

In the end it was Mister Clayton who found me rather than the reverse. I came upon a trail running through the underbrush. Stomping through the woods a shape lurched out of the darkness and threw me to the ground. It was not until I felt the pistol at my throat that I realized what happened.

"Mister Clayton?"

The dark shape shifted. "Charlie?"

I nodded. "What happened?"

"Lost him," he growled. The shape reached into its coat pocket and withdrew the flask. He tried to take a sip, but it was empty. Mister Clayton growled and tucked it back into his coat.

“What happened to your lantern?”

“Lost it.”

“What do we do now?”

“*I* go back to camp and try to suss out what to do next.” He stood off of me and walked away without even as much of an offered hand.

I pushed myself to a stand and began looking for my rifle. “And I?”

“Do what you want. S’your fault I lost him.” His voice was still unsteady. He walked fine, but his voice slurred. He stubbed his toe and stumbled against a tree. “Ow, Damnit!”

“I didn’t lose him!”

“You gave me away. I could’a shot him.”

“You went a-running after him your own self. Don’t pin this on me.” I came after him and tried to kick at him, but my short leg swung wide when he kept on walking himself out of range.

“Settle down, kid.”

I huffed, my breath coming short. I felt close to panic. “Settle down? *Settle down?* My father is dead! Whatever did it is coming after me now. You want me to *settle down*? I was told you could help me!”

He stopped. I didn’t notice until I ran into the back of him. In the dark I saw him pull off his hat and run a hand through his hair. He took a deep breath, gathering himself. I thought I heard him sniffle.

“Maybe if you weren’t so drunk all the time you might have caught it!”

Mister Clayton spun on me. His hands flexed and reached for my neck and I retreated a few steps. He took one more step toward me and stopped. Finally he slumped against a tree.

"No, you're right. Come on back to camp. But you ain't coming out on any more hunts."

I glared at him in the dark, but I followed.

Chapter 10

A Sacking

I woke before Mister Clayton by seconds. Dawn was still a way's away, the sky only just beginning to lighten. As I woke up I heard him stir in his blankets and his breathing lighten up. He gave a sharp snort and came out of it.

I lay in bed awhile longer feigning sleep while he got up and built a breakfast fire. I must have fallen asleep at some time because when the sizzling pop of breakfast frying caught my attention the sky was full morning.

We said nothing and I watched him cook from my blankets, knees clutched close to my chest. Mister Clayton's eyes were bloodshot and he kept pulling a ladle out of a nearby bucket of water to drink from it. His gaze never met mine.

When food was cooked he began to pour it out onto a plate for himself. He offered me some, but only grudgingly. I wouldn't have accepted—not from him—but I was famished.

Just so, the atmosphere of our little camp deadened the taste of the food. We ate in silence, Mister Clayton focused on his plate and I snapping furtive glances at him. Even in the state he was in his hand motions were precise and methodical.

While I watched, my eyes were drawn to a finger on his right hand. An insignia ring of some kind, iron by the looks of it. It bore a compass rose with a crude skull in place of the West mark.

“That’s an unusual ring,” I remarked, trying to clear the air.

“It is.” He said no more, and I made no more attempts at conversation.

The man’s yelps made the whores look up from where they hung camp laundry. I was walking past, carrying a bundle of goods from the company store bought with company money Mister Clayton had won in the Beaver. The noise was enough to make me stop in the street despite carts hauling lumber and other goods.

A wiry man was tossed from the whores’ encampment. He stumbled out of the tent enclosure and out into the mud, sending splatters up against the canvas partitions. A few passing men gave him a rough laugh. I could just make out the shape of Ginny’s head storming toward the partitions to come out in the street when I caught the wrong end of a cart driver’s whip.

“Make way, kid!”

I shouted more in surprise than pain and clutched my hand close as the cart stormed past. When I looked up again Ginny was wading into the mud arms swinging.

“—And if I ever catch you again it’ll be the last thing you ever see.” She grabbed at him.

The man stammered, lifted bodily out of the mud by his collar. “Buh-buh-but Ginny! I love her!”

“You don’t love her, Bean. No man does what you do can rightfully say he loves a woman. You threatened one of her regulars at knife point!”

“Now that’s not fair. The man was intimidating her.”

She raised a fist, “*You* intimidate her.”

He held his hands up to guard his face, though from here I could see the beginnings of bruises that said the damage had already been done. Though just as it seemed she might give him another slug across the face the Blue Beaver's proprietor came out into the street.

"You unhand him Virginia Catskill! That man is a paying customer."

She shook Bean, throwing a glare at House. "He's been threatening Gretchen!"

"And he still pays for her services. Now you gonna let her go or am I gonna have to make you?"

Ginny took Bean by the throat, still glaring defiance. "I'd like to see you try."

The proprietor just shook his head. "Suit yourself. Boys?"

Two men appeared from the crowd that had gathered. Large men with rolled up sleeves and unpleasant expressions. Ginny tossed Bean at one of them and tried to run. The second man caught her by the wrist and held her long enough for his companion to bat Bean aside and grab her other.

"What?" I cried.

House approached her. "You had this coming for a while, Ginny. You turned mean of late and I can't let my girls turn mean."

The beating was slow and methodical. The crowd watched in sick silence and I stood rooted to the spot unable to move. Through the crowd I saw the flash of a frock coat and a grey hat, heard the ratcheting click of a six gun's hammer drawing back broke the crowd's silence.

Samuel Henry Clayton stood not far off with the brass framed Remington trained on House' head.

"Three on one? That's hardly fair."

House paused, appraising the hunter. He sniffed, rubbing his knuckles. "No comments on beating up a woman?"

"I seen her. She can handle herself one on one. This, though…" He gestured with the pistol at the other two men. "This is just impolite."

The proprietor seemed to appraise his options. A bullet in the brain pan or…he shook his head and waved at the two men. "Alright, let her go."

Ginny stumbled to the mud, gasping. Her face was untouched—a kindness in her profession. House had been certain to aim every blow at her abdomen. She clutched it now, rolling into the mud to gasp for air.

He nudged her with a foot. "Get your things and go. You're done here."

She just scowled up at him. "You're ditching me? I'm one of your best drawing girls."

"You were. 'Til you started boxing my customers. Go, now."

Bean pulled away from the crowd. "My good sir, I want to show my thanks."

He offered House a handshake and House accepted. "Come by tonight for a free drink for your troubles."

"Oh, I will. I will." He peeked on his tip-toes at a blond woman, scared and weak-looking. "You hear that honey? I'll be by tonight."

Gretchen's face drew tight and she shifted to put one of the other girls between Bean and herself. House turned to appraise Mister Clayton. He gave the man a look of disgust, but hung over as he was Mister Clayton didn't seem to care.

Near me a man muttered in wonder, "Such a sight to see. She used to be so gentle, too. Ain't never had someone, whore or wife, who made love to me like Ginny Catskill."

I tried to catch Ginny before she was gone. I only caught a fleeting glance as she rode south on a horse. She gave me one last sad look and disappeared into the woods.

Chapter 11

Through the Woods

I returned to camp with my groceries and set to stowing everything in its place. Miles to the north I could still hear the knocking of axes against trees, and closer the occasional shrill scream of the mill. But closer still I became acutely aware of the quiet of local animals. No birds chirped, no creatures called.

Under the current of logging noise I could hear the current of the river. A cold sweat prickled on my brow. I looked nervously about me at the woods.

"Hello?"

I thought I heard something rustling in the underbrush. I quickened my pace, sweat galloping down my brown and the bridge of my nose. I blinked and some of it seeped into my eyes. I cursed and waved a hand at the sting. Too afraid to shut them both, I tried to look around with my burning eye, but my vision in it was blurry. Finally I clenched the eye and rubbed at it.

A twig snapped.

My eyes shot open and I looked around once more. There was nothing. I abandoned the food. If chipmunks got into it, then so be it.

I ducked out of the way of a wagon storming through the slush of the road as I crossed to the Blue Beaver and the bordello. A pair of women stood outside the Beaver, fanning themselves.

"'Llo, little Charlie," one of the girls said. "Ginny's gone."

Rather than meet their gazes, I stared at my shuffling foot. "I know. I was wondering if anyone had seen my father."

One of them took a long drag from her pipe, thinking it over. She blew smoke into the sky and said, "I think your old man was here talking to Laurel."

"Is—is she with a customer?"

She laughed. "Not right now. She's in the Beaver with House and Gretchen."

I nodded to them and moved to the saloon's canvas flap door. The oil lamps inside were all doused, but the room was dazzlingly bright. Light filtered clean and white through the roof, which was dappled with the shadows of the tree overhead—the lone tree standing in the camp.

There were no customers inside, just the three I'd been told of. Gretchen and Laurel sat in mismatched chairs at a table fashioned from planks and a wine barrel, sampling from a bottle with a far fancier label than any of the stock I normally saw the men drinking from. Laurel downed her pewter cup easily but Gretchen sat with her hands pursed in her lap, face blank, staring into the middle distance.

House paced around the table sleeves rolled up to bare impressive arms. He paused only when he saw me. "Private business, boy."

I stammered, but Laurel rescued me. "It's fine, Zachariah." She laid a hand on the bar keeper's thick corded arm. Judging by the somber faces, I knew I'd walked in on something unpleasant.

Laurel gave me a sweet smile. "I guess you found your pa, didn't you? Why didn't you tell me he was that tall drink of handsome wandering the camp? Gretchen, dear. Charlie is the son of the man what saved you from this morning's…events. What do you need, sweetie?"

Again I stared at my feet. "Have you seen him? Mi-my father?"

She glanced at Gretchen who was now looking up at me, and nodded. "Yes dearie. He came to see me a little after the—ah—incident this morning." Laurel gave House a frown at that.

"Did he say where he was going next?"

Laurel took a moment to think, clicking a fingernail against her teeth. "He asked me where the potter's field is."

"The graveyard?" I blinked.

She shrugged. "That is what he asked."

I thanked her for her time and started to make my way to the door. I itched to be out of that tense room. As my hand raised the flap House called out, "Hold up."

I stopped and turned to look at him.

"It true your old man is hunting the animal killing folk?"

"Yes, sir."

"Tell him there's a little extra money for him at the Blue Beaver, he ever kills it."

"I will sir."

As I slipped out the canvas flap something said inside caught my attention. After a moment's pause I slipped around the side of the saloon and came up on a shaded side where they might not see me through the half-canvas wall.

"Am I gonna have more trouble?" House asked.

Laurel said something I couldn't hear, and Gretchen muttered. I strained to hear what was said.

"—Will defend myself, House."

"He's got a free ride coming, Gretchen. Hey, hey now. None of that. No tears. What's wrong with you?"

There came the low, quiet and quibbling sound of Gretchen's weeping muffled by the canvas along with one last warning.

"If he tries to hurt me I will fight back."

The potter's field was on a rise east of camp, divided by a patch of trees protected from logging by their youth and scrawniness. I cut through the trees, scarcely fifteen feet high and few thicker than my wrist, and came into a small glade studded with wooden crosses and grave markers. The world fell quiet here, muted. Animals did not come close and the trees muffled the constant sawing and chopping of the workers.

The graves ran oldest to newest, front to back. The markers up front were listed five years ago or longer and were already bleached from long days of exposure to the Minnesota elements. As I moved further back the markers turned more yellow, the paint grew fresher, the dates moved closer. The dug graves grew fresher.

As I knelt to inspect a marker something shifted just out of the corner of my eye. I stood, turning to look. Mister Clayton paced in his shirtsleeves, cigarillo in mouth and his head swathed in a halo of light smoke, around a grave toward the back.

The grave was beneath the sole old tree in the field, a short but well spread oak tree. Branches thick with dark green leaves spread out over the lone marble marker. Mister Clayton paced there, thumb and forefinger touching his chin—a look I would later come to realize was his thinking look.

I drew close. "Mister Clayton?"

He turned his head to look at me. "Stalking me, boy?"

"The monster was following me." I suppressed a shiver. "I thought I should come find you. What are you looking at?"

Mister Clayton pulled his cigarillo from his teeth and gestured with it to the tombstone. "Somebody's been throwing a party out here. Heard rumors of a ghost—a figure in white. Don't think it's a ghost, though."

The tombstone was dribbled in wax, thick on top and running down the face of it. It pooled in several of the letters and dripped down the relief of an angel.

"What do you think it is?"

He shrugged. "Probably just a man and woman felling timber." I don't think he realized I could tell he was lying.

Something caught my eye. Carved into the dirt beneath the old oak tree I found a circle. The shape of it was most apparent, though at one time it might have had other shapes around and within it. Mister Clayton saw what I was looking at.

"Saw that," he said. "Whatever it was, it's a week old or more. Person made it ain't been here in some time."

The breeze shifted and with it came a new sound. Faintly I heard the ghost of the bell at camp ringing. I glanced to Mister Clayton and found him staring intently in the direction of the camp.

He dropped the stub of his cigarillo in the dirt and stomped it out with a sharp, precise motion. Without a word he ran, and I had to struggle to follow.

What we found, what everyone found, was the Irish foreman from the night before. I recognized the man by the remains of his clothes, but there was not much left otherwise to tell who he had been. He was found some miles north of town. The men said he'd needed to drop a load so he'd wandered off on his own. It was the screams that called them.

Mister Clayton and I stood apart from the crowd of gawkers. We shared a look, a conversation in a glance. Could someone be killing witnesses?

We remained when everyone dispersed. It was us two and the Company Man again. He mopped at his brow with a handkerchief, visibly greened by the sight. Myself, I did my best to never look in the direction of the body. I thought again unbidden of what Father must have looked like dragged into the water and I threw up in my mouth.

The company man watched us. Mister Clayton moved instinctually to the body and began poking through it. "This man wasn't drunk."

"How can you tell?" I asked.

"I can see his lunch."

A gob rose in my throat. "I'll—I'll look for tracks."

The search didn't take long. A slab of granite lay in the ground partially grown over by grass a few feet from the body. There, deep in the rock was a mess of paw prints as clear as if they were stamped in mud. I called to Mister Clayton and he came, the Company Man following close behind.

"Those must have been there all along," the company man said. "Must have. I have a cousin who went west in forty-nine. Said he found monstrous dragon's footprints embedded in rock. Ancient."

"Sure, ancient." Mister Clayton didn't look up from the prints. He pressed his fingers into one of the impressions. The paw was massive. Bigger than his hand.

He traced the course of the paw prints. They mingled close together, often pressing into each other as if the creature had walked the area over and over. Blood from the corpse stained the closer ones. It gave a clear indication that whatever killed the man had left the prints.

He continued to study the prints until finally he stood up and dusted off his knees. "Creature went south after eating." He pointed lazily down past the logging camp.

"It couldn't have been the animal that left them in the stone," the company man swore again. Mister Clayton said nothing as he walked past the man and mounted his horse.

I began to trot after him and eventually he reigned up watching me. "I think I told you, you weren't joining me on any more hunts."

I thrust out my jaw and planted my hands on my hips. "You help people, right?"

He turned away from me and nudged the horse back into movement. I kept up with him.

"I said you help people, don't you?"

"I hunt monsters. Not the same thing."

"Then help me hunt my monster and I'll leave you alone."

I thought I perceived his eye twitch. "I can't—I'm not—look, child. If I don't solve this as soon as I can more people will die."

"So you do help people." I crossed my arms, nodding thoughtfully. "It's just like the man in Springfield said."

"What man? Who did you talk to?"

"Just some rail worker. He said you were a great man. That you saved his life. Samson seemed to also think highly of you, though I don't know why."

"What do you mean you—" He held up a hand. "You know what? No. I'm not getting into this. Follow me if you want, but if you get dragged into some monster lair I will not be held responsible."

I gave a thin smile and followed along, jogging beside the horse.

He kept an eye out for more granite outcroppings, and I helped. Slowly we began to piece together the movements of the creature. Every so often we would find the scrape of a claw or a print stamped deep in the rock. Never would there be so much as a bent leaf of grass, though. It did not seem to leave its mark anywhere but in stone.

Finally toward dark the trail went cold. We found one last paw print but nothing to follow it up. Mister Clayton lit a lantern and held it high, peering around. "Few miles down and we hit the bluffs. Might'n be living in one of the caves down that way." He pulled the Henry out of its saddle scabbard and dismounted.

"We go the rest of the way on foot. Woods are getting too thick out here."

We had just begun to move again when we heard the scream. High, thin. It sounded like a woman.

"Could be a fox," I said.

"Ain't a fox," was his reply. Without another word he passed the horse to me and took off at a trot through the woods. His pace was slowed by the dense undergrowth, but we took what speed we could.

Noise doesn't carry in the woods, so he knew we had to be close. It wasn't maybe a few hundred yards and around the side of a far hill when we found a shape darting through the woods. Ahead of me I watched Mister Clayton drop to one knee and size up the shape down the sight of his rifle.

I recognized Bean not two seconds before Mister Clayton fired.

I wrenched the gun by the barrel a moment before it fired. The gun bucked violently in my hand and smacked me across the face. My knees buckled under the blow and I nearly collapsed.

Mister Clayton cursed, but to his credit he lowered the rifle. A moment later Bean swept through the woods towards us and Mister Clayton nabbed him out of the dark. The man was breathing hard, his eyes wild. He cast his gaze about, searching.

"What is it?" Mister Clayton asked. When the man didn't answer he shook him. "Answer me!"

"C-cat!" he stammered.

"What kind?" I asked.

Mister Clayton was no longer watching Bean. He stared off into the distance, beyond the lantern's glow. "Big kind."

My eyes followed his out into the blackness. It was out there among the trees, circling us. True to the dead foreman's words, it had to be as big as a wagon-maybe bigger. It moved with a serpentine grace, paws not even disturbing the deadfall and underbrush. Plate-large eyes glowed from the dark with a baleful yellow light, and its pelt was reddish orange, covered with sinuous black stripes. I recognized the form out of a book I'd read once upon a time, in a different life.

"Mister Clayton, that is a tiger."

"So it is."

The tiger paused, weighing us. Mister Clayton did not allow it a moment longer for thought. Mister Clayton dropped the lumberjack into the dirt and rolled to one side. With a sweep of his hand he raised the Henry.

"Run."

Before we could register the order he fired. Bean scrambled to his feet and I was not far behind.

The horse vanished into the woods away from us. We fled over rock and root, but the dark and the woods impaired our way. Several times I tripped or crashed into something unseen in the dark. Light bobbed behind me, and foolishly looking over my shoulder I saw Mister Clayton following after us.

Behind him loped the tiger. Tree and rock were no obstacle and it encroached on us too quickly. Mister Clayton nearly tripped, snagged on something unseen. His hand flailed out, swinging the lantern wide.

The tiger balked at the swing, coming up short. It was all he needed to catch his balance again. He pushed off of a tree and took flight once more.

I stumbled into a bramble and screamed. My momentum was lost, and a thousand needle points pierced me. The footprints of the tiger pounded close, and in panic I ripped myself free of the bramble and fell into a creek.

Water splashed into my bramble cuts and made my skin feel like fire. Thrashing and crawling, I pulled myself out of the creek on the opposite bank just ahead of the tiger. Bean was long gone but Mister Clayton was waiting for me.

He stood over me, lantern held high. On the other creek bank just out of arm's reach paced the tiger. Mister Clayton stared at it, and it stared back. It walked up and down the bank, throat rumbling a low growl.

With infinite patience Mister Clayton set the lantern down and pulled out his Remington, checking the rounds. He slipped the cylinder back into place and looked back to the Tiger.

The tiger crouched low, considering us. Its tail twitched back and forth as it tried to decide what to do.

"Why isn't it crossing?" I asked.

He said nothing.

"Why aren't we running?" I asked, louder. I realized the creek was there and I squeaked, jumping back from it. Frantically I started brushing at the water and my damp clothes as if that might ward off the river-thing.

Mister Clayton ignored me. He squatted over the lamp studying the tiger. The two watched each other like old men over a chess board. Each tensed at the shoulders, each ready to strike. Each seemed to challenge the other to make the first move. The size of the creature was beyond scope. Its head alone was the size of a steamer trunk.

We waited. The tiger waited. My pulse hammered against my chest, anticipating the moment the tiger would lunge and end us. I'd end up torn and ripped up like the other victims—like a potato sack.

After an eternity the tiger snorted with disgust. He turned and began to slink off. But not before looking over his shoulder with those burning eyes and warning us. "You're next."

Then it vanished into the dark.

Chapter 12

Two Kinds of War

He finished tending to my scrapes by light of our campfire. There wasn't much to do, but he checked the bad ones for infection and patched them up. Then when we were done he went back to a set of bags he didn't commonly keep on his horse. From within he pulled out a stuffed and worn leather bound book. It was tied shut with twine to keep the contents in.

"What about your horse?" I asked. He didn't seem terribly upset, but the loss weighed on my conscience.

Mister Clayton shrugged, sitting down by the fire and untying the book. "He's a good horse. He'll find his way back here by morning." And then he fell silent, slipping easily into whatever the book had to convey.

He flipped pages from time to time, skipping ahead or doubling back on where he'd been. Occasionally he'd grunt surprise or confirmation. Once he snorted. I didn't know what to make of that.

"What is that you are reading?" I asked, tentatively.

"Research."

I gingerly let myself down into the dust beside him. "You are trying to find out what that creature was?"

He grunted again and scratched at his face where an old scar cut into the cropped beard on his jaw.

"What is it?"

Mister Clayton closed the book, marking his place with a finger. "You gonna keep asking questions?"

I swallowed, but timidly I nodded.

He closed his eyes for a moment—a kind of *Lord Give Me Strength*—and finally looked at me. "What we're dealing with is a spirit."

"A spirit? Like a ghost?"

"Different. Usually spirits represent something."

I frowned. "Like what?"

"Law, love, anger, intellect. There can also be spirits of a place, of a thing." He ticked off each example on his fingers. "Lots of kinds."

"So what was this one?"

"Unsure." He opened up the book again and fell into it.

"How did you know it was a spirit? It looked pretty solid to me."

"They can be. Just gotta have something pulling them here." He put the book back down, resigned that he wasn't going to be able to read it. I watched him as he pushed himself to his feet and put a new log on the fire.

Staring in the fire he answered my other question. "It was the crick."

"Crick?"

"Stream. Spirits can't cross flowing water."

Water again. I, too, stared into the fire now. I contemplated what he told me. "Could someone cause a spirit to be here?"

He said nothing.

"I mean…tigers do not usually live in Minnesota and you said something's gotta call it here right? Can a spirit be called? Like a—" I searched my memory, the books I'd read. Faust came to mind. "Can it be called like a demon."

Mister Clayton peered at me across the fire. "You're actually a pretty sharp kid."

I looked down to hide my blush. “Father encouraged me to read. He wanted me to be a doctor when I grew up.”

“You got a doctor’s mind alright. Have to, to suss all that out.” He flipped through a few pages and turned the book to me. Long ago someone had torn the page from another book and pasted it in place here. The paper was a slightly darker tan, and showed a faded woodcut print. The woodcut depicted a dark night, forks of lightning cutting the sky. Beneath a coven of men and women danced around a burning circle in the ground—a circle marked with an intricate geometric shape. And rising from that circle was a powerfully built man.

“That circle we found earlier,” I said.

He nodded and went back to his reading.

Silence fell between us. The night air buzzed with crickets and frog song. A fox barked in the distance.

“Does your book say what killed my father?”

It was his turn to avoid my gaze. He picked a stick off the ground and played with it for a few moments before tossing it into the fire. He seemed unsettled.

“My book doesn’t say much. Had to write some friends, get a little information. I think it’s a nix.”

I frowned. “What is a nix?”

“Surprised you don’t know, being a kraut. They’re river fairies. The men—nix—are all ugly. The girls, though? The nixe? Beautiful. Siren-like. Girls lure folk into a river and drown ‘em. The men just drag people under. Result’s the same. I think they like their food drowned the way we like our food cooked.”

I said nothing, thought nothing. I could hardly breathe.

He sighed and stood back up. As I watched he walked a circuit around the fire, restless.

"Why does a nix want me dead?"

"Florian told me a story. Back in the old country your folk lived by a river. Some fool got it in his head to strike a deal with the river's fairy. Fortune or luck or something. Maybe gold. The nix just cares about food—told them to give up their first born every generation."

I watched the fire. I could picture everything in my head, though I'd never seen the Fatherland. I knew almost nothing of the Kirchner clan beyond what little I knew of Florian Kirchner, my father.

Still, the image came full. The millstream and the mill. The man and the nix shaking hands. I knew well how the nix would assure fortune for the Kirchners: people standing in their way must have had a funny habit of falling into the stream.

Mister Clayton spoke again. This was the most I'd ever heard him say at once. "He ran. Or so he told me. Left home when his time came, and was always just a step ahead of the nix. Thought he'd lost him when he crossed over."

I frowned. "But he still asked for your help?"

"Asked me to keep an ear to the ground. Told me of his problem."

"Is that how you met?"

Mister Clayton shook his head. He pulled a cigarillo from his case and bit the end off. He leaned toward the fire, face first, to light it.

"There was bad business at that vineyard he worked at. That's how we met."

I frowned. That made sense, though. I remembered there was a point when father had been afraid to return to work. That must have been why.

He smoked at his cigarillo for a long time without saying anything more. I guessed that he was finally dry on words.

"How do we take care of the tiger spirit?" I asked.

He pointed the cigarillo at me. "*We* do not." Gesturing at himself he said, "*I* will hunt down the summoner tomorrow. Just need to find tracks again."

I began to protest but he stood up and began to pull out his bedroll.

"*You*," he pointed at me again, "will get some sleep. Kitty wants us now. You're helping watch. Two hour shifts. I'll wake you when it's your turn."

I thought of protesting but kept it bottled. I returned to my bedroll and climbed under the blankets. While I did he pulled out a bottle of whiskey to go with his smoke.

"Good night, Mister Clayton." I frowned at the bottle.

"Call me Samuel." He avoided looking at me when he said it, and the words were so quiet I wasn't sure I heard him properly.

"Good night, Samuel."

"Sleep tight, Charlie."

The bottle was empty when the time came for me to take my shift. But the night sky had changed too much. I realized as Samuel curled up under his blankets that he had allowed me to have more than just two hours' sleep.

The fire had burned low so I put more wood on and sat down to watch. Samuel snored lightly and didn't stir much in his sleep. When I was finally certain he was fully asleep I crept to the saddlebag and poked through it. Amidst dozens of vials full of strange powders and liquids and dried plants I found the book.

I untied the book and sat by the fire to read. The first page bore a stamp of that symbol on Samuel's ring: a compass rose with the western demarcation replaced with a skull. Below a flowing and graceful hand had written, *This Charlotte Bible is dedicated for Samuel Clayton. May you find the peace you seek.*

That drew a curious frown. *What is a Charlotte Bible?* I asked myself. I read on. The book was written in many different hands, and was littered with loose papers containing addendums or corrections. Inside I discovered what dime novels today would call the *preternatural.* Back then, we just called them monsters.

There was the anatomy and battle tactics of troll raiders. There the names of demons and the incantations that would banish them. There were a hundred kinds of fairy including my own tormentor the nix. Revenants could be killed by beheading and hurt by mustard seed. Ghosts could be slowed and made physical with bone ash. Fairy creatures were mortally wounded by cold forged iron.

I found the section about Nix (Nix; Nixe; Nixie. Neck; Neckar). There was not much to know other than what Samuel had relayed. The page looked newer than many of the others, written in what I'd come to realize was Samuel's cramped and tight hand. And tucked within the page was a poem on a small scrap of paper.

Where by the marishes boometh the bittern,

Neckar the soulless one sits with his ghittern.
Sits inconsolable, friendless and foeless.
Waiting his destiny,—Neckar the soulless.
—Sebastian Evans 1865

On the next page I found a folded letter in a much more familiar hand: my father's.

January, 1870

Mister Clayton,

I am writing to inquire upon the things of which we spoke. Have you made progress? I hope your associates have found something of use for my situation. Of late I have experienced nightmares, and while I do not have any evidence to support this, I believe the time is drawing near that the creature will find me. I shall write again should I begin to suspect that it has found my son and I, but I would appreciate the time to gather with you and talk about what you have learned. Are there any protective measures I should take? Your diligence in this regard has been greatly appreciated.

Warmest regards,

Florian Kirchner, Hermann Missouri

A knot formed in my gut. I felt a dam's pressure of unshed tears about to break, but somehow the dam held. This was written mere months before father's death and he would never get the chance to write warnings to Samuel about the nix's return. I glanced at Samuel where he lay sleeping and folded the letter, tucking it into my pocket.

I needed a distraction from my own grief. I continued reading. A thousand wicked creatures stalking the periphery of human vision, and almost every entry carried a means of countering, stopping, or slowing them. Whoever the authors of this book were, they worked with Samuel. They helped people.

I regarded the sleeping man again. He twitched fearfully, the bottle beside him empty. This broken sot of a man was actually a hero, though I knew he refused to think of himself that way.

"No, no," he muttered in his sleep. "Turn back, they're opening fire."

A veteran of the war, then. I was suddenly reminded of the man at the Beaver calling him Johnny Reb. Samuel made no pains to hide his Kentucky accent, so his former allegiance would have been obvious to anyone.

I went to my bedroll and took my blanket to him. As I laid it across his shoulders his twitching seemed to subside. The muttering stopped, but every so often as my watch continued I heard a quiet sob.

A soldier of two wars, each unnatural in its own way. I'd seen the men returning home to Hermann after the war ended. They were destroyed, to a man, even if they hadn't been killed bodily they might as well have been.

I kept my watch by studying the book. This world fascinated me. According to the book there was more out there than Heaven and Hell—there were things between. There was no room for superstition, simply what was and what was not. Science, though Samuel might be insulted to see it regarded as such.

When the first hints of dawn came I put the book back in the saddlebags and woke Samuel.

"You let me sleep too long," he said. He reached for the bottle, but rolled his eyes when he saw it was empty.

I squatted beside him, studying. "You did the same for me."

"You looked tired."

"So did you."

He continued to grumble, but didn't make anything of it. By the time the sky was lit I was cooking breakfast while he retrieved a bucket of water. We were steeling ourselves—there was work to be done today.

Chapter 13

A Burning Question

Samuel went to work shortly after breakfast leaving me to do the cleanup. I didn't dare go near water so when the bucket was empty; I wiped my hands on my filthy britches and said, "That is as clean as they get."

Following the usual "safety in the herd" mentality I went back to the logging camp. Armed, of course. Samuel had taken both of his revolvers and the Henry but I still had my Sharps. As always the logging camp was empty but for those working in the offices or the mill. The countryside rang, rattled, and chopped with the hard work of the rest of the camp.

I watched the women of the bordello for a while, wishing I had a chance to see Ginny again. A short distance from their tents many of the women were hard at work scrubbing and hanging clothes. Their life was a hard one—I could see it etched in every scar, every bruise, and every sag and wrinkle. The nature of their existence proved itself in the guarded ways they moved and the subdued banter between girls washing and girls hanging clothes.

Laurel was talking to the quiet and worn Gretchen while they scrubbed clothes against washboards. "Has he been by since?"

Gretchen shook her head. "I have not seen him since last night. I do not like the man, but I do not hope he was a victim."

That caught my attention. As I walked over to them they both looked up. Laurel smiled, but I could see Gretchen frown as she considered my rifle.

"Li'l Charlie," Laurel said by way of greeting. "When are you going to tell your handsome daddy to come by?"

I gave a shy smile.

Laurel chatted, but I did not hear her. My attention drawn by Gretchen who was studying me. She seemed wary, but in retrospect I suppose there is much in the kind of life she lived that would make one distrusting of men. She finally nodded, yellow hair hanging limp in her face.

"It is a kind thing your father did for Ginny. She was good to us, until the end," she said.

I wasn't sure what to say so I gave a small voiced, "It is—he is a good man. Most of the time."

She frowned again, gazing down at her work, furiously scrubbing the brown out of a white shirt. I saw her brows crinkle just a little. "I wanted to ask you yesterday. Your accent—your father does not speak like that. Are you German?"

A lie caught. I covered my panic with a sniffle and concocted another lie. "My mother is—was. She and father, they met in Boston." The last part was at least true enough. She nodded, accepting it.

"We met many Germans along the way here. My family is—ah, I am Norwegian."

I nodded, unsure what to say. A question flitted on the outer reaches of my mind so I gathered up my courage and asked it. "Have you heard from Ginny?"

They gave me a curious look. Laurel was the one to answer. "She only been out of the camp a day, Charlie."

"Right. Right." I looked down at my boots, nudging a toe through the mud. "Everyone says she *used* to be kind, *used* to be gentle. She seemed—" I caught myself short of saying, 'Beautiful,' or perhaps, 'Wonderful.' "She seemed very kind to me."

Laurel hitched her shawl up over her bare shoulders, squinting at the sun. "Most days she is—was." She frowned to herself. "But she weren't cut out for this life. Don't know what she did before Minnesota but it weren't whoring. Sometimes you get Johns, they're so wound up it makes 'em aggressive. You know what I mean?"

I didn't, but I nodded anyway.

"Well anyway. Sometimes they get a touch mean like. She endured when it was her, but she loves big. Hates to see anyone she cares about hurt. She started storming in and hitting back. Or snapping at people. Couldn't understand why we just took it—never mind she did just that."

Something nagged at the back of my mind. The seed of an idea forming. Bean's terrified face as he ran from the Tiger formed there beside that little niggling something.

"Were any of the men who died mean to you?"

Laurel paused. Gretchen said nothing. They both seemed to sink into their thoughts for a while.

Gretchen asked me in her quiet voice, "Did they find Bean? Is he dead?"

I couldn't meet her eyes. "He isn't. But he almost was. Samu—father came in at the last moment."

Laurel bounced to her feet, taking me by the shoulders. "Last moment. Did he—did he kill the critter killin' all these men?"

All I could do was shake my head. "We distracted it, though. It chased us instead."

"I should have said yes," Gretchen said. The words hung in the air, soft as they were and I saw guilt begin to draw her face down.

Laurel shifted her attention from me to her friend. "Now you knock that off. You ain't obligated to marry the first man as stalks you."

"Maybe he would be good to me."

"Fool man thinks just because he's nice to you, you owe him a poke. We all seen what he's like when pressed. He won't be good to you. If you won't believe me then believe Ginny."

I began to back away. The knowledge burned me. Ginny was the summoner. I tried to picture her with the cat. An image formed in my head of the woodcut in the Charlotte Bible, of Ginny among the men and women dancing around that burning circle.

"Charlie?" Laurel asked. "You alright?"

"I need to go talk to father."

"You tell us when you find that animal again, alright?"

"Alright."

I ran off before they could say anything else. Past carts and wagons, past men returning for a break. I was half way through camp before spying something through the window of the survey office. A map hung on the far wall detailing every rise, ledge, stand of trees, and—most importantly—every single creek and body of water. My pace slowed to a halt and another thought occurred to me.

"If the tiger cannot cross moving water, and if it is attacking at the camp, there is only so many places for the summoner to hide!"

I moved to the window, looking furtively this way and that for anyone who might be watching. Secure in my privacy I stood on the tips of my toes and peered through the dusty glass. A man with compass and protractor stood over a cluttered and messy desk staring down maps. He made marks and adjustments occasionally referencing a this stack of books or that sheaf of papers.

Something must have caught his eye, as I saw him start to look up. I ducked below the sill again, breathing hard. The map. I needed that map. Inside I heard the bark of a chair scooting back. I clamped my mouth to try and settle my breath and bolted around the far side of the office. I hid there between the surveyor's office and a canvas tent serving some other administrative function.

From my side of the wall I heard boot steps make their way to the front door and step down the small stoop. I did not hear him walk back in, but a thousand heartbeats later I heard a triangle ringing in the lunch crowd. From my little hiding spot I spied the surveyor leave to get food.

My opportunity was made by a conveniently timed meal.

I bolted into the office and tore the map from the wall. I tried folding it down but found that did nothing to help. Would there be no way to sneak this into my pocket? Of course not, not something this big. Rather, I rolled it up and hoped no one would notice.

A cloud of hungry workers, like locusts, could be seen from the window walking down the road to the cook tents. I stepped out of the office and melded into that crowd, ducking and weaving the press. I was carried south with the throng, toward the mill and the edge of town when a hand snatched me from the stream.

She pulled me to the side of the mill and pressed me against the wood. A hand lay against my mouth, muffling my startled screams. Ginny Catskill. She gave an impish smile and inclined her head. I do not know how the men in that crowd did not see her. I do not know how *I* had not seen her before now. But here we stood in broad daylight with God and everyone around us, and she just grinned at me.

Ginny lifted her hand from my mouth and gave me a peck on the cheek. "Hello, little Charlie. You did not tell me your father was a hunter."

Did I spy a manic twitch at the corner of her lips? I could not be sure. I *cannot* be sure. Even today I do not know how much wildness was present and how much was my imagination.

I shrugged one shoulder and tried to play it off. "Well, you know. He moves from camp to camp taking care of wolves. I think he was a trapper once."

Her smile turned more crooked and I tried not to swallow.

"Is he getting close to finding this wolf?"

How much could I tell her? "We think it's a cat, actually."

"Oh, there's nothing to be afraid of with little pussy cats. Scratch under their chin and they're yours to command."

"What are you doing here? They kicked you out of camp."

"I still had some things to take care of. You know how it is." She gave me a pat on the cheek with one hand and slipped something into my palm with the other. "It was beautiful to talk to you. Take these—think of them as good luck charms."

I looked down at the charms. Each was a small cloth sachet tied with twine. I could feel twigs poking from inside, and the brittle feel of dried leaves.

"Two," she said. "One for clever Charlie and one for his handsome daddy. Put it under your pillow at night and you'll have pleasant dreams."

I nodded slowly. Maybe Samuel would know what they were. Maybe they weren't even dangerous. I slipped them into my pocket and looked back up at her. And perhaps that gleam in her eyes wasn't dangerous either.

Ginny gave me another kiss on the cheek and waved goodbye. While I gawked she climbed the steps to the mill and disappeared inside.

My head buzzed when I walked away from the mill. The crowd had gone, though, and progress became easier. One of the brothel girls was walking toward the sleeping tents with a basket of freshly laundered clothes when she saw me. The woman gave me and the map a look, raising a curious eye.

"Your pappy's up at the Beaver if'n you're still looking for him," she said.

True to her word I found him when I stepped through the canvas flap. Samuel stood at the bar opposite of Zachariah House, a bottle between them. Both men looked up as I entered. A bindle lay open with its contents scattered over the bar top.

"Charlie," Samuel said with an affability that I found unnatural coming from him. "Stopped in for a drink?"

"You're drunk," I said.

"No," he replied and picked up the bottle. "But this should help."

I tucked the map by the door and went over to them. It took more effort than I'd have liked to get my short legs up onto the barstool. The effects spread out over the counter were obviously feminine: a stack of letters in a flowery hand, a coin that seemed to be pressed from lead, some ribbons for hair, and a bundle of dried flowers.

"These were Ginny Catskill's possessions," House explained. "Someone busted in last night and took some of 'em."

"'N I have an interest in anyone who is interested in Ginny Catskill," Samuel said. With a precise hand he picked up the bottle and poured a finger for himself in a fat cup. He inspected her things and I helped, poking through the letters. Many of them seemed to come from enamored clients, but I found a few sheets that all seemed to be the botched beginning of the same letter.

Dearest Momma,

As I write this I have traveled far north and west. You may be pleased to hear I am currently living in a new-minted state! I have found employment in Minnesota and intend to stay here fore awhile. The work is not what I would have expected, but there are few roles for women in the frontier. To answer your previous letter, I have kept my book and kept it safe. And I have kept faith, and kept in practice. I feel the danger of these lands and the men about me, and I study with a fervor I know Cunning Orpah would have wished I possessed back home. ~~*I confess you would disapprove of my work*~~

The letter stopped there. The others were the same. Each made the same oblique references to practice and study, the same references to danger. And each stopped when Ginny had tried to explain the nature of her employment.

A woman appeared at a flap door beside the liquor cabinet. “House, I think Mercy’s missed a period.”

“God help me,” he muttered. Then he turned back to us. “Be right back, gentlemen.”

When House was gone I proceeded to relay to Samuel the day’s events. He waited until I was through, breathless to the end, and asked a few pointed questions but seemed to really consider what I was telling him.

My heart thudded the whole time. I didn’t want to believe that she was the summoner. The touch of her hand had been so warm and she had been so good to me and so beautiful (and I was just the kind of foolish boy to equate beauty to goodness back then). On the other hand, evidence grew.

“If we were to ask around I bet you every single man dead would probably have been mean to the girls,” I finished.

“Or near enough of them as makes no difference,” he said. He scratched at his beard and looked off into the distance. He nodded and patted me on the shoulder. “And if we were to look in her things before someone swiped them,

I suspect we'd find a spell book. Good work, Charlie. You confirmed what I was beginning to suspect."

I beamed, feeling as though he'd stuck a blue ribbon on my breast.

"Stay here, in camp. I'll hunt her down. You said she was at the mill?"

I felt my pulse freeze in my neck. "What? Samuel, no. She's a good person."

"She's a killer." He began to stand but his knees betrayed him and braced himself against the bar. His drinking hand's precision did not seem to apply to his legs.

"She was just defending her friends!"

He pushed past me, his hand dropping to the butt of the Remington at his side. "Can't summon these things without them feeding back on you."

I jogged after him, tried to get around in front of him and stop him. "You help people!"

I nearly had him blocked but he swerved around me, clipping my shoulder as he past. I stumbled a little and fell into the floor. That tore it. My lip began to wobble and my eyes began to burn.

Samuel turned slightly at the first sign of a sniffle. He looked on the verge of apology but he shook his head. "I told you, kid. I'm not good enough to help—I'm just a killer."

"Then maybe it was a mistake for me to come to you!" I pulled myself up by a table.

"Maybe you shouldn't have."

I couldn't see for all the tears in my vision and I knocked an unlit lamp from the table trying to stand. It collapsed to the floor with a clatter and a crash, sending oil and shards of the globe across the wood planking. When I looked up Samuel was starting to bend over to help pick up the pieces. Incensed, I kicked his shin rather than take his help. He danced back cursing loudly.

"You want it like this?" he hissed. "Fine. Go your own way."

"Maybe I will!"

"Go on, then!"

"And you go on! I don't need your help. You'd just get sloppy drunk and shoot yourself in the foot. Wouldn't even know it was Ginny if it weren't for me."

He tried to say something. His mouth worked soundlessly, his blue eyes burning cold. Finally Samuel turned away from me and out the door. Through the flap I saw a small crowd attracted by the shouting. Men had seen us. Women had seen us. I felt a touch on my shoulder.

Gretchen stood by me while Laurel knelt picking up glass pieces. They must have come in through House's back entrance. I shrugged her off. She pulled back a little and Laurel was there to put an arm around her shoulder. They both gawked, struck by the look on my face.

"Charlie, you alright?" Laurel asked. "What was that about Ginny?"

"It was nothing," I muttered. It sounded like the pouting of a foolish child in my own ears. I turned away from them both and ran.

Chapter 14

Killers

No one followed me back the short distance to where Samuel camped. I swung a wild kick at a pebble, wanting to take this rage out on something, anything. To my disappointment the rock didn't go sailing miles into the distance. Despite the rage I poured into the kick the rock scuttled maybe five feet and stopped.

I screamed until my voice went hoarse and collapsed onto my blankets, kicking and punching at the blankets and the ground. As I rolled to one side I felt something crack in my pocket. Squirming, I positioned myself on my back and stuffed my hand into the pocket. There where I'd left them were the two charms Ginny had given us.

Was she sincere, I wondered. Did she really wish us well? Perhaps if she was a genuine witch they had some power to keep us in good health. I set mine by my things and threw Samuel's into the dead fire pit.

Petty, I realize.

Obviously I couldn't stay with Samuel. I was no longer welcome. Not after everything we'd said to each other. If I kept traveling I would still be hunted by the nix. I doubted I would even make it out to the waterless tracts of the far west. Of course I would have to end the fight sooner rather than later.

It would have been impossible for me to hear the river as far as it was, much less with the droning sound of the mill upstream. That whine carried for miles around, even beyond the range of the axes and saws further north. Still, I was sure I could hear it—the passive burble of the river. It sang to me, seduced me to strip down and climb into the water. There I would meet him, there he waited. He would die, or I would die.

I've always been a fatalistic, melancholic soul—even as a boy. Do not interpret my actions as those of a child sure of his invincibility. Rather, I was certain that one way or another things would end here and now. My resolve steeled, I took my Sharps and loaded it, and made sure I could easily draw Samuel's knife. Better safe than sorry, I decided. Thus prepared, I marched a mile east toward the river.

The sound of the river only became audible when I drew within a hundred feet. The cold black water of the St. Croix kept a lazy pace carrying bark and leaves down river. Occasionally I saw the silver flash of a fish snatching a bug from the air but there was no visible trace of the nix. But even without seeing it, I knew it was there. I could feel its slimy gaze on me. I suppressed a shiver and sat down on a rock with the rifle on my lap.

"Just try me," I muttered in German. And there I waited.

And waited.

And waited, still.

The afternoon bugs were singing when I heard footsteps behind me. I cocked the hammer on the Sharps and stood, spinning in place. Samuel stood by the side of a tree, rifle slung over his shoulder. His eyes seemed bloodshot, though I doubted he'd been doing any crying.

"The hell are you doing out here?"

"Waiting for the nix."

He tongued a bead of saliva to his lips and spat. “You trying to get yourself killed?”

I thrust my jaw out defiantly. “No, I am trying to kill *him.*”

Samuel eyed the Sharps. “Take more than that to kill him.” His eye wandered down to the knife at my belt. He pointed at it. “That’s mine.”

I turned my back on him and sat back down on the rock. “Did you come to apologize?”

“Come to tell you to leave the camp.”

“Why, so you won’t have to see when the nix kills me?” Even I was disgusted by the petulant tone in my own voice. A second later I felt his hat swat me over the head.

“Stupid boy! I’m warning you off because your lady-friend wants us dead.” He was shaking something in his hand when I turned to look at him. It was the little burlap charm bag, grey with ash—the one I’d thrown in the fire pit.

“How do you know those have anything to do with Ginny?”

He fingered the lock of hair tying the bag shut, the color of autumn and copper. “Witch bag. Put ‘em where the victim sleeps. Kills you in your dreams. The maker has to tie it shut with her own hair to finish the binding.”

I couldn’t help rolling my eyes. “That sounds dumb.”

“But frog fairies, ghosts, and phantom tigers don’t? You’re already neck deep in this mess, son.”

He had a point. I squinted at him. “Ghosts?”

“You said you talked to Samson didn’t you?”

I nodded.

"Charlie, Samson's been dead for three years. He protects my land from the townsfolk."

He had my attention now. I scooted on the rock to face him. Samuel came to stand beside me, staring out at the river. He squatted there and laid the Henry across his knees. "I need you to leave town. Once business is done here I'll come meet you."

My voice was quiet. I tried not to speak the fear that held me. "The nix will kill me before you can reach me."

"No he won't."

"Yes. He will." The feel of the creature's oily gaze had disappeared. For the first time in hours I felt safe. "You don't have to kill her, Samuel."

He picked a pebble off the ground weighing it in his hand. Standing, he flung it into the river and we watched it skip across the surface. A fish tried to snatch it out of the air.

"I do, though. Summoning's two ways. Spirit does what you want but it touches you, too."

"That's not possible. She was good to me."

"Boy, I'd wager she was the first pretty young thing to say hello to you after running for your life."

My cheeks burned but I wouldn't tell him he was right.

He continued. "You heard everyone. She's gotten meaner. It'll only get worse."

"We can warn her off."

"She done already tried to kill us both. She'll be too far gone."

I fell quiet.

“I don’t help people, Charlie. Most time, by the time I get there too many already died. All I can do is kill monsters.”

“But you’ll help me?”

He hesitated. “I’ll try. You staying in camp?”

I nodded.

“Alright then. Get up. Let’s put some distance between us’n the water.”

We walked away together, and I thought somewhere behind us I heard the angry growl of a bullfrog.

Chapter 15

Best Laid Plans

Late that afternoon we passed through the logging camp on our way out. Things were dying down for the day and lights already burned within the Blue Beaver. Men gathered around the bordello waiting to hand in laundry, waiting for a bath, or waiting for love. I eyed the crowd, but Bean was nowhere to be seen.

Samuel moved with long strides and I had to work to keep up with him. His head was wreathed in a cloud of smoke which trailed as he walked and he seemed lost in thought. Though the moist summer air clung to me and made me roll up my sleeves, he seemed untouched by anything.

"How do you kill a spirit?" I asked.

Samuel sniffed. "As well kill an idea."

I furrowed my brow, trying to make sense of what he said. "So what do we do about the Tiger?"

"Banish it and tackle the summoner."

I kept my voice low, looking around. "How do we banish it?"

He held out three fingers and began to tick them off. "One of three ways usually: certain plant smokes, burning salt, or fire."

My head tilted and I frowned. "Only one of those? How do we know which?"

"Luck."

My frown deepened. I thought it over. We passed near the mill, now quiet after a day's long work. Movement caught the corner of my eye and I turned my head. I just caught a flash of white dress vanishing into one of the side doors.

Samuel stopped. "Something wrong?"

"Uh?" I shook my head. "Oh. No."

He studied me for a heartbeat and glanced at the mill. Shaking his head he turned heel and began walking again.

I caught back up with him. "What about—ah—her?"

His voice was also low, just loud enough for me to hear. "Witches work with three things: a book, a rod, and a circle. Break the circle or deprive her of book or rod."

"Then we can talk to her?"

"Then we can kill her."

When I said nothing he looked over his shoulder at me. If I hoped for some apology in his eyes I found none. They were hard eyes, cold. The eyes of a man who had done such before and would do such again. I swallowed a gobbet stuck in my throat and decided I would most certainly keep the thing I saw at the mill to myself.

"Fire," I said.

"Hm?"

"The Tiger fears fire. I saw it balk when you swung your lantern at it."

For the second time today he appraised me with a favorable glance. "Sharp eye." The surety of his gaze told me he had caught the same. "We'll have to deal with the Tiger tonight."

"Why is that?"

"Won't take her long to realize we found her witch bags. She'll bring out Tiger next."

"What do we do now?"

"Follow me."

The night woods sung with life. Crickets and frogs worked in chorus while owls triumphed over their prey and foxes barked in the night. And still our footsteps sounded too loud to my ears. Deadfall crunched underfoot as we moved through the moss-smelling dark, a lone oasis of lantern light. We were coming around the half-way mark on our second circuit of the woods surrounding the camp.

Samuel held the lantern above and away from his head with one hand, the Remington gripped loosely in the other. I stayed not far behind clutching the Henry. It was loaded with three special bullets.

"These are the last of what I've got," he'd said back at our camp as he slid three into his Remington and three into the Henry.

"What are they?"

He thrust the Henry into my hands, not looking up as he set to work checking his pistol. "Salt rolled into the lead. Burns when you fire the powder." After a brief inspection he stood up and holstered the revolver. "Plan B."

"In case Plan A doesn't work?"

"In case Plan A doesn't work," he agreed.

Now we walked circles in the woods on the alert. My eyes strained at the dark trying to see further than the little light would allow. Oh to be able to see as owls see, I told myself. Every few feet we stopped and listened. As I listened I noticed something: sound by sound the forest was falling quiet around us. First the birds and the foxes disappeared, then the frogs. Then at last went the crickets.

"Samuel?" I asked in a voice far too fretful.

"I know."

We halted. Both of us turned slow circles, taking in the landscape. The ground around us dipped and waved in small folds and wrinkles instead of lying flat or stretching out into larger hills. That would be treacherous. The tree roots and deadfall would only increase problems.

I fixed my grip on the rifle. Would there be a sound? Would there be a warning?

"Run," was all Samuel said.

He bolted. After a moment's hesitation I followed. The lantern bobbed and swayed ahead of me, always telling me where to run. Samuel's own shadowed movements gave me some small warning of the dangers underfoot. I tripped and stumbled, but I never fell.

"Go! Go! Go!" he yelled.

A whisper of breath caused me to look over my shoulder. Out of the black stormed the Tiger. Larger than life it drew closer and closer.

Blood pumped hard in my neck and my lungs screamed with every breath. I tried to shout but the breath wouldn't come.

The air cracked, shattered. That pulled me out of my deadly fear. Ahead of me Samuel aimed the revolver at me. Behind me the creature roared, falling back a few paces.

"Hurts him!" Samuel shouted. "Shoot!"

I fumbled as I ran, trying to aim over my shoulder. I couldn't get a bead on him. My bullet went high and wide, and I thought the beast smiled. His teeth gleamed and his glowing eyes narrowed.

Ahead of me Samuel stopped. "Keep running!" We were in a clearing now. Not a manmade clearing, but a natural one with grass running up to my knees. He leveled his gun hand and again the night shattered with gunfire.

The Tiger shrieked, leapt toward us.

Samuel's teeth flashed in a rare grin. "Got you, son of a bitch." That was when he threw the lantern.

The ground before us flashed into hot, angry fire. Our preparations worked—kerosene and dead grass laid out in a circle caught immediately and the growing flames trapped the Tiger within.

He roared, screamed in pained agony, and I saw white smoke lifting off of his form.

"Keep an eye on him, Charlie. Make sure he don't escape!"

The fire flashed, grew. It seemed to feed off the Tiger. He curled up, pained, and began biting at his own limbs as if he could put out the flames. Jagged, angular webs of holes began to burn through him. It was like watching a dry leaf catch fire.

The flames intensified and I threw an arm over my face. I felt Samuel grab my collar and pull me back. Hot air flashed across and three stripes of pain crossed my arm.

"Stay back!" Samuel shouted.

I stumbled backwards, gripping my arm. My jaw worked, but I could make no noise. Pain seared and I felt blood well between my fingers. Samuel shot into the fire and I saw what happened. In the brief second I'd averted my eyes the Tiger had launched forward and struck at me.

If it were not for Samuel I would be dead.

Samuel stuffed the Remington into his holster and held out a hand. "Rifle." I passed the Henry to him and he chambered the next round with a flick of the lever. I clutched my searing, screaming arm close. Samuel would be distracted by the Tiger. The Tiger was almost done with. Holes were crumbling through his form, showing shining white light within.

Samuel fired again as the Tiger tried to slip out of the fire. A hand sized section of the Tiger's flank collapsed inward where he struck. "Wrap your arm," he said without passion.

"What?"

"Take off your shirt, wrap your arm."

The bleeding. Right. I began to do as he said, quickly pulling off my filthy, ripped shirt. It was clumsy, but for the moment it would do. My arm still burned and I could feel the shirt turning wet. But I was alive.

The fire was quickly spreading beyond the confines of our little circle. In the far distance I heard the alarm bell of the logging camp. Men would be coming soon. Men would be distracted from the mill. And Samuel…he was distracted with the Tiger.

I ran.

Behind me the Tiger sprang, leaping out of the fire. Again Samuel opened fire. A flash of light briefly lit his furious face. He screamed at me to come back and the Tiger fell out of the air. He would be fine, I told myself. He would be fine.

Chapter 16

Endings

I clutched my shirt-wrapped arm close as I ran into camp. What men I saw ignored me. Everyone rushed toward the fire in the distant woods. The mill was dark when I arrived. It stood, imposing itself above the bank of the river. A foundation of river stone stood up to my chest, and the wood was built on top of that. The smokestacks of the steam engine stood lifeless, and the finger wide gaps between the planks of the walls were black.

Sweat and blood clung to my skin, cooling me despite the heavy, moist summer air. I hunched my shoulders close, shivering only a little as I opened the side door where I had seen her enter. A tarp lay over the river side entrance where logs were hauled up a ramp from the river. Troughs ran the length of the building toward the massive saws, and fully half the back of the building gave way to a great steam engine. Orange embers still glowed in its massive boiler.

My footsteps were oddly muffled and when I looked down I saw the floor was thick with sawdust. Footprints pressed in the dust wandered everywhere, but mine were clearer than the rest. There had been no new dustfall to obscure them. Besides mine though, I saw another pair that seemed a little clearer. Sawdust choked the cracks between the tightly fit floorboards, but every so often a patch fell through and faint yellow candle light trickled up from the gaps.

“Ginny?” My voice croaked oddly. My muscles ached with the stiffness of terror. I was shivering, but it was no longer from the cold.

The footprints led me toward the back of the mill house. I took each footstep cautiously—I could hear the river’s flow loud in my ears, a reminder of what other dangers might be waiting in the dark. In a far corner of the large room behind a stack of freshly hewn lumber I found the hatch. The footprints led straight to it and disappeared.

I called out again. “Ginny, are you there? It’s Charlie. I am coming down.”

I thought I heard a groan below me. I stifled a noise of terror and pulled the rung on the hatch. It swung open easily and I let it rest on a crate. I took a deep breath, peering into the maw, and contemplated what dread thing might be waiting down there for me. The nix’s bulbous eyes flashed to the front of my mind.

A number of stairs descended into a hastily carved crawl space beneath the stone foundation. Shadows played, tossed by the flicker of a candle’s flame. I had to duck my head to keep from knocking it against floor joists and machine parts dangling from the low ceiling. The mechanisms linking the boiler to the saw all ran down here beneath the floor. Like above, saw dust coated much of the floor mixing with dirt. The confined space smelled rank, of exposed river clay.

My eyes moved toward the light beyond the saw. A small tunnel carved through spider and cobwebs clinging from the joists and machinery. I crawled, feeling the web silk draping against my clothes, clinging to me. I tried not to think of creatures hitching a ride on my back. The crawl was perhaps fifty feet, but it felt a mile in that enclosed space. At the far end, likely below the door where I'd entered, I came out into a widened place.

It was here that I found the circle, lit by a lonely pair of candles melted down to stubs. Light fell weak around the space and the dark seemed thick, ready to fall on me like a blanket. The circle itself was carved into the clay of the river bank, sharp and clear. Geometric symbols dissected the interior into a dozen smaller spaces and all around the exterior edge were small angular glyphs—characters in a language I did not recognize.

A dark leather-bound book lay in the center of the circle, spread open and face down in the wet clay. It seemed dropped in a moment of haste. Gingerly I cross over the circle, smudging lines with my hands and my knees. I picked it up by the spine as gently as I could and looked at it. At first glance I felt like I was looking at Samuel's Charlotte Bible. The page in question, wet and smudged with clay, was pasted in. It had been torn from a different book.

In an instant I recognized the circle depicted on the page—it was a twin, glyphs and all, to the circle I crouched in. Above that was a block of text, smudged and bleeding from the wet. My gaze traveled past the unreadable text to the header:

SPIRITUS RETRIBUTIONIS

I mouthed the words, then said aloud, "Spirit of retribution?"

My hand swept over the muddy, damp text trying to clear away some of the obstruction, but the damage was done. Unless Ginny had the spell memorized rote no one would be using this page again.

A small gasp to my side caused me to reel, nearly dropping the book again.

Ginny curled in on herself against one wall, her face hidden in shadow and her body taking shuddering pained breaths. I could see cuts, bloody gouges carved along her arms which she held close to her body. She stirred as I crossed to her.

"Ginny?"

The sound from her throat was feral, bestial. I paused.

She spoke after another gasp. "I could feel it." Her voice came broken. It sounded a struggle for her to speak. "I could feel it when you banished him."

I hesitated, and when I did she mumbled, "Broke my wand."

I began cautious toward her again, but she shrieked at me. "No closer! No. No closer." She sobbed. "Why did it have to be you, Charlie?" Her crying voice shuddered, heaved. It warped and twisted, growing into a mad cackling laugh.

"You banished him and I can still feel him in my head." Ginny gave another choked laugh. "Up high in the air he jumped, he did. And that bullet burned, oh Charlie it burned. Burned him right away. Nothing left but a thought." She tapped her temple with finger and giggled.

There were gouges in her face near that temple. I could see black blood dried under the fingernail. She wiped at her nose, dragging sticky dark blood across her face like the stroke of a grotesque artist's brush.

Sometime during my distraction the alarm bell outside died. There was no sound now but the water, the distant singing of summer frogs, and Ginny's intermittent laughter and crying.

"Ginny, come on. Come with me. You need to leave here." I took another step.

She shot forward on all fours, moving faster than seemed possible. I threw up my arms over my face and felt her crash past me. I scattered to one side into the dark, tearing through webs.

The sound of struggles filled the air. Grunting, cursing, inhuman growls. The small space exploded with the sound of a gunshot.

I clutched my hands to my ears, ringing filling my head. Curling on my side I could see the struggle across the space. White on black, Ginny wrestled with Samuel at the foot of the stairs. Her dress muddied and bloodied. She wrenched his arm unnaturally. A sickening pop pierced the air and Samuel screamed.

"Stop it!" I shouted. "Stop fighting!"

She was on top now. She straddled his chest with her knees pinning his arms at painful angles. In the shadowed flickering dark I could see her start to deliver blow after blow to his face, snarling, growling. I scrambled onto all fours and rushed the two of them.

My good hand grasped at the collar of her dress. She didn't pull away when I tugged but the distraction was enough. Samuel reached into his belt and drew something. The knife in his hand threw candle light.

Ginny tossed an arm back and strength beyond her size threw me off of her. My ribs creaked under the blow and I tumbled away from her. As I watched she snatched the knife from Samuel's hands. The knife rose high in the air, and as it fell I screamed.

He tried to roll. He jerked, moved. But I saw it, saw the knife plunge home.

Samuel gripped the knife where she pressed it into his side. It wouldn't budge. Ginny sat over him, snarling, grinning triumphant. Even in the dark I could see the dark flower of blood blooming across his shirt.

So he punched her.

The blow wiped the vicious grin off her face. She reeled back with surprise. It was enough. Roles reversed. The knife was out of his side and in his hand. Faster than I could track he plunged it deep in her chest.

Ginny struggled against him, wrapped her hands around his neck. But even as she did he pulled it out and stabbed again and again. Blood rose on her lips and dripped onto his face. Blood trickled out of her chest, down over his knuckles.

She began to sag. Her breath came, sticky and wet. "You—can't be rid of me that," she coughed, a racking and consumptive noise. "That easily."

Samuel began to squirm, to try to pull away from her but she gripped him by the neck. Her other hand darted to the hole in his side and pressed. Samuel screamed. Her thumb withdrew from him, wet, and began to draw on his shirt. A circle, symbols.

I fought through the webs, tried to reach them. Ginny began to speak again. This time the words were not

English. It was a whispered, sibilant tongue who's meaning seemed to slip to the left or right of me any time I thought I grasped it. I felt a pressure in the room, the air the moment before lightning strikes. The hair on the back of my neck raised, waiting for something awful.

But that was the end of it. That sentence pulled the last of her strength. The pressure faded, and so did she.

Ginny Catskill died. The world fell quiet.

I scrambled back over to where they lay. My sides ached and my arm burned, but I could still crawl.

As I drew close Samuel groaned. "Get her off me."

I helped him roll her off. He curled onto his side, taking stock of his body. "Knife wound's pretty bad." By the light of the fire I could see his face taut, drawn. Beneath the bruising across his face and neck he looked infinitely sad.

"Your face looks awful," I offered.

"Helpful. Tear that shirt up, would you? Need a bandage."

The world as dead as Ginny Catskill when we limped out of the mill house. His side and my arm were both bandaged. We paused, aching, and looked up at the sky.

"She tried to kill me." My voice was hushed, dry.

Samuel shook his head. "No, she came after me. Didn't want to hurt you."

I frowned at him, brows furrowing. "You really couldn't save her, could you?"

He said nothing, just watched the stars overhead. Idly he began to wipe the mud off of his Remington, recovered after the fight, onto his shirt. When he was ready to speak again he took a deep breath.

"Need to take care of the body. Before anyone finds it."

"Is it always like this?" I asked.

"Damn near." Satisfied with the job on his pistol he reached into his coat and lit a cigarillo.

I tried to shake the image of Ginny's lifeless body sinking into the river. A involuntary shiver took my body, but only felt a single tear roll down my cheek. I was mourned out. I cleared my throat and Samuel glanced at me.

"You did not drink anything tonight."

"So I didn't." Samuel quietly puffed at the cigarillo. "Let's rest a spell and we'll get to work."

In the distance I could still see the light of the burning woods.

The job was done. The river took her quickly, pulling her beneath the ice cold snow-melt. Our limbs moved more easily now, the aches starting to melt under use. My arm still burned, but it hurt less. I could tell every motion hurt Samuel but he neither complained nor asked me to take up his slack. I think he didn't want to leave such a gruesome task to an inexperienced boy.

As we walked away from the mill I noticed a crowd gathered around the bordello tents. When I stopped Samuel stopped too. Together we drew close, but we didn't need to be so close just to see the commotion. My throat closed at the sight and I heard Samuel spit beside me in disgust.

Laurel hung by her neck from a tent pole, eviscerated. Her guts spilled in tangled red ropes to the ground, and though flies had not yet gathered the stink of her was unimaginable. Someone had painted a message in her blood on the canvas partition. Great red smears spelled out three words in German.

KIRCHNER COME HOME

Chapter 17

A Rough Trail

I stared at the pommel of the stolen horse's saddle. The landscape changed around me, woods giving way to broad sweeping seas of grass, but I could pay it no mind. The events of the last twenty four hours still played over and over in my head.

The campfire, heating the needle under Samuel's supervision and threading it with catgut. Sewing his skin shut in his side. Watching, *feeling* the needle pass into his flesh. Walking through the crowd gathered around the remains of Laurel, seeing the grin of rictus terror upon her face and smelling her rank innards spilled upon the dirt. Watching Ginny barrel toward me with mad eyes, watching her stab Samuel. Watching Samuel snuff the light out of her.

God help me, I thought I could actually see the light fade in her.

I fell off the horse, my shirt dampening with morning dew. I crawled a few feet away and my whole gut heaved. For the umpteenth time that day involuntary spasms wracked my stomach, my chest, caused my shoulders to curl in on me. Nothing came up but a few dabs of yellow foam.

"You're going to keep thinking about it," Samuel said. He was not riding his horse. Not with fresh stitches in his side. He wore a new clean shirt taken from his bags, without any of the blood, dirt, or sweat of the logging camp on it. He passed by.

A moment later Samuel returned. He offered a cloth damp and cold and helped to wipe my face off. In his other hand he held a tin mug of water.

“Drink.” He urged the cup into my hands

I thrust the cup away just seconds ahead of a fresh wave of spasms and dry heaving. I convulsed and stared at the ground, spewing air until the wave subsided. Beside me I heard Samuel whisper something to himself.

“You say something?” My voice croaked, reminding me of Nix. That reminded me of Laurel. To my surprise no third wave of dry heaves came.

“Hm? No.” He thrust the cup on me again. I took it this time. The water stung my acid burned throat but I could feel it loosening the knots in my stomach. At the bottom of the cup I had a long slow exhale of breath. It misted in the morning air which was surprisingly cold for summer.

“Need to rest?” Samuel asked.

I’d had to push his shoulder back into place and stitch up his side and he was asking if I wanted a rest. Shame burned in my cheeks and I shook my head. He helped me to my feet and we walked back to the horses.

Whispers pulled at my attention again. I turned, looking around me. Morning made the dew sparkle on the tall grass and the dark shapes of birds could be seen lighting off from distant patches of woods. But there was no one else around us.

“Samuel, I keep hearing things.” I turned back to him, but what I saw made me take two steps back.

He hung from his horse’s stirrup by one hand, gripping his side. Red was blooming on the white of his new shirt and staining his fingers. I rushed to him and helped him to the ground. Beside us the horses danced nervously, snorting white plumes of breath.

"Samuel! Samuel, mein Gott, are you alright?"

"Stitches," was all he said. His voice grated and he winced. I pulled the shirt out from his pants and belt and tugged it up. Every last stitch I'd sewn into him was cut, looking as if a knife had run along the wound and neatly snipped each. I helped him out of his shirt and quickly balled it up, wadding it against the wound.

"What do we do?" I could feel my blood rising, panic setting in. "Samuel, what do we do?"

He gave a pained grunt, shifting on the ground. "Get me comfortable. Need to sew it back shut."

Bile rose in my throat. "Y-yes. Yes, of course."

I set him back up with his bedroll under his head and built a fire as quick as I could. Trying to get the wood to light was maddening. Every time I almost had a spark a cold breeze would come along and stamp it out. On two occasions I tried to get something from the saddlebags only to turn around and see the fire had gone out again. And when I would turn back to the saddlebags they would be re-belted and stuck.

"Lilac," he muttered. "Got one bundle of lilac left in the bags. Light it, wave it around."

"What? Why?" I stared at him, but did as he asked. The belt straps were stuck, but they opened after some doing.

He narrowed his eyes. Already I could see his skin turning white, sweat breaking out on his upper lip. "I see you Ginny Catskill, and damn you to hell for what you done."

I found the sweet-smelling roll of lilac in the same bag as the rest of his apothecary goods. It was rolled in brown paper which I ripped off. Quickly, with shaking hands, I fell by the side of the fire and tried to relight it. The flint and steel kept sparking but the wood wouldn't light. The ground was too wet and the cold wind too strong.

Every time I would put my back to the wind it changed direction. Frustrated, I began stacking the wood around the tinder and my hands. I struck again, and again, and again. Finally something lit. Kneeling in, I blew on it gently. The flame came to life—not much, but enough to light the lilac.

I came away with a smoldering, smoking bundle of lilac.

"Wave it around," he muttered.

I did as he asked. As I watched the wind died. The air warmed around us and color began to return to his face. Samuel pulled the wad of his shirt away from the knife wound and checked it. Blood scabbed and turned black. There was some oozing, but nothing that couldn't be cleaned. The bleeding had slowed to a manageable level again.

"Time for the sewing," he said. "Get the whiskey."

It was worse the second time. Now I had to pick my old stitches out. When the sewing was done I let him rest. We ate a mid-morning brunch and he dozed for an hour while I flipped through the book. I wasn't sure what happened and didn't even know where to begin looking for it, so I just read. Two hours on Samuel woke up and took the book from my hands.

"We'll need more lilac. You remember what it looks like?"

I nodded.

"Good. I need to go easy on these stitches. You're hunting it down. Get me a half dozen more bundles like the one you burned just now." He threw a buffalo chip on the fire and wiped his hands in the grass. "I see any game I'll shoot us up some supper for tonight."

It took two hours of searching, but I was able to pull up what we needed. I returned to camp with six small bundles of lilac and let him tie them up with twine and tuck them away. We rode off again, restocked and with two rabbits hanging off his saddle for dinner.

Over the next two days I had to redo the stitches three more times. Each time was preceded by whispers and cold—and each time the stitches looked like they had been snipped with an expert's hand.

Afternoon of the second day we came upon a small river town where a steam boat was taking on passengers. Samuel bought two tickets for St. Louis and collapsed in our room.

Chapter 18

Hermann

From Iowa to St. Louis, and then on down to Hermann the trip moved much more quickly. We had to replace our stock of catgut in St. Louis due to the mysterious stitch ripping, and I continued every other day or so to have to sew him back up again. At the least I can say the act no longer made me nauseous. I wondered if perhaps father had been right to peg me for a future doctor.

Even with rooms and warm beds Samuel insisted we take turns keeping watch at night. Nightmares wracked the man, and on several occasions I had to shake him awake from something that set his body convulsing and his breathing raw. Often, he took longer than agreed-upon watches and let me sleep while he stayed awake. I wondered then how he did it, but I have since grown and learned the pain-defying powers of a good bourbon—and Samuel always liked a good bourbon.

When it came time for my watch I would curl up in a chair in the corner of our cabin. At night something walked the hallways, and while it was likely a porter I always wondered if it might be something else. Whenever I heard these footsteps my grip on the Henry tightened.

We sweated it out, managed to survive the journey by boat. The small boat we took passage on for the second leg of the journey finally came to rest on the bank of the Missouri which home overlooked.

Hermann is a town of hills. One side of the bank is flatlands, floodplains suitable for a little bit of farming. The other bank, though—hills swept up from where the water touched land and created great rolling shapes. As a child I'd always imagined the vineyards, the grass, and the woods as a kind of blanket laying over some great giant. The hills were the wrinkles, the folds, the shape of his knees and his body while he slept.

The smells of steam engines mingled with the smells of hearth smoke, and the further distant smells of grapes and woods on the wind. I took a deep breath as I stepped off the gangplank, only just realizing how my home smelled like nowhere else I'd been. Out of the corner of my eye I caught Samuel watching me, studying my face.

"It feels very good to be home."

He just smiled.

We made our way through the men working the docks. We were the only passengers getting off here, but there was still cargo for the men to load up. Already bare chested men were rolling great barrels of wine up the gangplanks and onto the boat.

"Where do we go now?" I asked.

He appraised the town. Two and three story red brick businesses crowded side by side to exposed frame German houses. Samuel tapped his foot on the ground, thinking.

"Shouldn't camp outdoors if we can help it. Nix'll be waiting for us."

A frown tugged at my mouth. "Do we have to stay at my house…?"

He considered me for a moment. Mercifully he shook his head. "No, I don't think so. Know a place to stay?"

Frau Sackoff stood pinning sheets on lines to dry as we rode up to the boarding house. She looked tired and wan, and I noticed a coach gun propped against her laundry basket. She caught sight of us as we came near and poked her head from around the side of a great white sheet.

"Charlie?" she asked. "Charles Florian Kirchner, bist du das?"

"Hello, Frau Sackoff." I dismounted and tied the reins to a nearby birch tree. She picked up her skirts and almost ran to me before sweeping me into a big hug.

"Charlie! Christ's holy blood I thought you were lost to us. I saw your letter, but what happened? The whole town was talking about it."

"Maybe I will tell you some time."

Samuel glanced at me and I realized I would probably have to act as translator for most people here. It had taken me no time at all to settle back into the familiar Rhinelander.

"Ah—this is Samuel Clayton. He is a friend of my father's."

She offered her hand to him, speaking a broken kind of English. "Any friend of Florian's is welcome here." She regarded the two pistols at his belt and the scabbarded rifle on his saddle.

"Frau Sackoff, what happened?" I looked around. Her bushes were trampled and I noticed the fence looked worse for wear. "I've only been gone a few months."

"There is some kind of animal prowling about. Drags our animals away, terrorizes people in their homes. Folk are saying it's a cougar or a rabid coyote but I have seen it." She leaned in close to us, conspiratorial. "It walks like a man."

Samuel waited for me to translate. I passed what she said to him.

"We're…" I paused, not sure how to put this. "Frau Sackoff, can I tell you a secret?"

She nodded.

"I believe you. The creature you're talking about is what killed father. I brought Samuel here to help me with him."

Samuel's shoulders visibly tensed. "I heard my name. What did you tell her?"

Frau Sackoff addressed him directly. "Do you—eh—hunt these?" She pantomimed firing a rifle.

He gave me a long suffering glance that promised a stern talk later. "Yes, ma'am. That is correct."

"Come in, then. Come in." She waved us in, sweeping up the stoop into the house. She spoke German again, "I have only one room left open. You are fortunate you came when you did."

"Your house is filling up?" I asked.

"Some of the vineyard workers—the single ones—they want safety in numbers."

When we were situated in a room Samuel took a slip of paper and wrote on it. He folded the paper and handed it to me.

"What is this?" I asked.

"I want you to take this down to the blacksmith. We will need a handful of these made. Tell him I will pay well."

I frowned. Boat tickets, boarding house, and now whatever this was. "Does monster hunting pay well?"

"Not especially."

"Then where…?"

"No time. Go. Meet me back at your house when you're done."

Coming home was a strange feeling. The house looked derelict. There was a hole in the roof over the bedroom, perhaps left by a passing storm. Windows had been broken out with rocks and the door left hanging open. The holes, the door, the windows—everything seemed impenetrably black inside. For a ghost of a moment I wondered if the shade of my father would come storming out to drag me with him to the afterlife. A lump caught in my throat and I had to take a deep breath and swallow.

"Found some powder and wadding in the house for your Sharps." Samuel caught me in my own mind and surprised me. He was stripped to the waist, baring his bandaged midriff to the world. A bag hung from the haft of father's old pickaxe, swung over his shoulder.

"What about your rifle?"

He jerked his head, a motion to follow him, and led me around the side of the house. "We'll have that too. Need the Sharps, though."

A shovel stood upright in a pile of dirt. He had evidently been busy. I peered down in the hole. It went down probably four feet and water glistened in the bottom.

"No good." Samuel sniffed. "Need a dry hole."

"Why?"

"Fairies often have strange powers around their element."

I pursed my lips, realizing where he was going with this. "And he's a water, you said?"

"River."

"Right." I looked around for a moment, assessing the area. "We could go up the hill."

He followed my gaze up the hill and away from the river. The woods cleared out halfway up around a flattened area. He nodded. "That was my thinking. Come on."

The boarding house echoed with life in the morning. Bleary eyed men bustled about getting ready for the day's work or coming home from a late night out. Before the sun was even up the sound of footsteps in the hallway woke me. I laid awake in our rope frame bed listening.

I shifted, rolling onto my back. Samuel was still awake from his watch, pistol on the night stand beside him and the Charlotte Bible open in his lap. He nodded greetings when he noticed me.

"Sleep well?"

I sat up, shrugging. "Did you sleep at all?"

"Dozed a little. Get used to sleeping light when it's just your own self."

The next room over a man was cursing in thick German. Samuel snorted.

"You understood that?"

"Cussing's obvious—in most languages at least. But…" He shook his head. "Your whole tongue sounds like a bar fight."

I got ready for the day, pulling on my britches and suspenders over the shirt I'd worn to bed. A little water splashed on the face, and I was ready to go. Samuel had never undressed. He simply laid his hat on and pulled on his gun belt.

We only saw a handful of the other boarders on our way downstairs but they eyed Samuel and his pistol, leery. Even Frau Sackoff's dogs seemed suspicious. They got up from where they lay on a rug in the sitting room when we came downstairs, one of them whining at the sight of him.

In the kitchen I could hear her muttering to herself. I walked in, closing an open cabinet door for her as I did. Frau Sackoff crouched before the oven, cursing to herself.

"Is there something wrong?"

She jumped at the sound and laid a hand on her chest. "Oh, Charles. It's just you. Yes—no. I keep lighting this God be damned oven and it keeps going out on me."

"Did you check the flue?" I asked.

She managed to get the logs lit again and closed the door. "Six times." As she stood up she looked over my shoulder. She walked past me and closed the cabinet I had just closed a moment ago—somehow it had opened again. "Bother, I was sure I'd closed that cabinet. I'm not sure where my mind is this morning."

"Could we bother you for some breakfast, Frau Sackoff?"

She smiled and patted me on the shoulder. For Samuel's sake she switched to English. "There is cheese on the table and bread with some honey or liverwurst if you prefer. And you, Herr Clayton? I have some coffee if you would like." She looked over my shoulder and I followed her gaze.

Samuel stood in the sitting room doorway and I could see already his face was calculating. I knew he was sizing up the stubborn cook fire and the re-opening cabinets, but he said nothing about it. He nodded slowly to her, his voice quiet.

"Thank you, ma'am. Do you know if any men here are looking for a day's work? I'll pay."

Chapter 19

The Trap Laid

The sky was blue in the way that Missouri skies often are—hazy, thick with water, and threatening rain. We stood on the hill overlooking my house by seven o'clock, judging by the bells of St. George. By Missouri standards it was a beautiful summer Saturday morning. The breeze brought a sigh of leaves from the cottonwoods and the smell of someone nearby baking bread.

Karl Jorgensen, a man who worked only occasionally on the docks, was more than happy to volunteer for Samuel's offer of three dollars for a few hours' work. Generous by any means, I knew Samuel just wanted the work done quick. Samuel dispensed instruction to Karl and I ("I want a hole dug. Five feet wide, ten deep") while he settled down in the grass with the package retrieved from the blacksmith.

"What is the hole for?" Karl asked, scratching at his lice-ridden beard.

Samuel looked up from laying out the blacksmith's order and raised an impatient eyebrow. "A well."

Karl looked at Samuel, then to me, and then down the hillside. I knew his line of thinking. Who the hell would dig a well on the side of a hill?

Karl and I dug and occasionally Samuel would come by to inspect the work, peering down into the hole at us. "Walls need to be smoother," he'd say. Or "Dig faster, I'm not paying by the hour."

The first hour we worked Samuel took the blacksmith's package—six dull grey balls—and methodically converted them into six paper cartridges sized for the Sharps. When that was completed he grabbed an axe from the house and began chopping limbs and sharpening them into something resembling spears. Karl's eyes bulged when he saw that.

We finished near noon. Karl was a fast worker and was able to make up even for my weak arms. We climbed out of the hole on a rope tied to a tree some ten feet from the hole and broke for lunch.

He eyed Samuel's pile of sharpened stakes nervously. "If I did not know better I would say you were planning to kill a tiger." He forced a chuckle.

Samuel slowed only for a moment in his preparations, fixing Karl with a flat stare until the other man's chuckles died on the breeze. After lunch the man was paid and went on his way, shaking his head.

I sat across from Samuel, wolfing down some cold sausage and cheese packed for us by Frau Sackoff. The cartridges sat upright in a paper box waiting to be loaded. I gestured with my bread.

"What did you have the man make?"

"Iron slugs. Your rifle is smoothbore, so they'll actually fire."

I frowned. "Why iron?"

"Fairies—hurts them. Poisons like lead, but worse."

"Fire hurts spirits, iron poisons fairies." I began to wonder about the anatomy of these creatures, how they were so alien from our own. "Who discovered that?"

He took a brush and began to scour out the barrel of the Sharps, inspecting it as he cleaned. "The English. But somewhere along the way someone sussed out it don't just work on English faeries."

I finished off the sausage, leaving only the taste of spice and salt on my tongue. I found myself licking my fingers to get the grease off. Samuel gave me an irritated glance.

"Need you working. Cut down some saplings. Need eight, 'bout my height with lot of leaves."

A few hours later I returned with saplings in tow, mostly birch but with a few elm. While I was out he laid the spikes in the ground at the bottom of the pit and pulled himself out. As I returned I saw him clutching his side, and for a jarring moment I was scared the stitches had snipped again.

"Side just hurts," was all he said to me. For the pain he took a swig from a bottle of brandy, ignoring my frown.

We wove the saplings into a flimsy cover to lay over the hole. Branches went atop it, and grass atop that. It wasn't beautiful, but it wasn't easily visible from a distance off. If I was very careful I could walk across the top of it, but the covering creaked with each step. I didn't dare take more than a step or two out.

Evening came on us slowly. The setting sun found the two of us down by the house building a fire for the night. He set out a pot to boil coffee and I helped him skin a rabbit to cook.

I watched him tuck into the rabbit, the ring catching my eyes again. I took a cautious nibble at the rabbit, burning my tongue. Samuel offered me a cup and I took a swig without checking it just to cool my tongue. My mouth and throat filled with a burn as I had never known before and I spat the poison into the fire. The fire thanked me with a small flare up.

Samuel cackled as I wiped my mouth on my sleeve, slapping his knee. "Never had brandy before, have you?"

My scowl was answer enough. He rinsed out the cup from the water bucket and poured me a ladle of cold stream water by way of apology.

Samuel made a show of blowing on his haunch of rabbit to cool it. Again I looked at the ring and finally asked, "Is the person who wrote your book the same one who gave you the ring?"

His eating slowed. He took a longer moment to chew his food, staring into the fire as though he looked there for a way to answer my question. Finally he swallowed and took a breath.

"After a sort. This bible is a collaboration between me and some other men."

"Monster hunters?"

Samuel fixed me with a queer look and shook his head ruefully. "I suppose that's the way to refer to us. Man who brought us together had these rings made. Represents our mission."

I frowned and took a bite of rabbit. It was gamey, but well-cooked and pleasantly greasy. Chewing it gave me a moment to think. "What's your mission?"

"Take a guess."

A group of monster hunters, then. Before I could think of what I was saying I asked in a small voice, "Could I join?"

Samuel waved a hand as if swatting the idea from the air. "Out of the question. This is a terrible life, lonesome and dangerous."

A fire ignited in my chest. Perhaps it was the swallow of brandy or months of stress manifesting as defiance. "And why not? At least I'm not drunk all the time. Why are *you* good for it?"

The haunted look that came over him then, I will never forget it. His eyes glistened in the fire light which shadowed his face. He seemed inscrutable to me. Alien.

"Because I'm good for nothing else."

I said nothing, could say nothing. Bands of regret gripped my chest and I pulled my knees to me and stared into the fire. Samuel, likewise, stared into the fire. The sound of crackling and popping replaced our banter. After a time he pulled the Sharps to hand and wandered out of the firelight to piss. I threw a rock into the dark to vent my own anger.

When Samuel returned his eyes shifted this way and that, scoping the darkness around us.

"Keep sharp." He picked up the bucket and dumped it.

"What was that for?" I had just started to want for a drink.

"Don't want our friend listening in on us." Samuel picked up a fresh log and some lavender to throw on the fire. "And I need you awake. It's time to be bait."

Samuel stayed close through the night, with no trading of shifts. We were both committed to stay awake as long as necessary. Every time I started to nod Samuel prodded me.

"Get up, walk a couple laps around the fire."

I'd nod, though sleepy as I was it was really more of a barely controlled bob.

The second time I had to pace I studied him while I walked. His face was drawn tight, and purple bags hung under his eyes. The untrimmed beard lent him a wild, melancholic appearance.

"You've not been sleeping," I said.

Samuel grunted.

"When I take watch I hear you muttering in your sleep."

"S'nightmares is all."

"They're getting worse. You weren't sleeping like this up in Minnesota."

He began to rub the back of his neck, letting out a slow, rasping breath. "Just remembering some things I'd rather not. Apparently a bad time for it."

I squatted across the fire from him and tried to warm my hands. "You were a soldier, right?"

He paused, frowning. Samuel mulled over how he would answer for a moment and said, "Kentucky. Served various units, mostly cavalry."

I nodded. It fit with what I'd heard him muttering. I supposed his hat was his old cavalry hat, minus patches and decoration. As I watched Samuel pulled his arms close and shivered. His head bobbed a few times, but he pulled through it and stayed awake. His eyes were rimmed red, but I didn't think it was the alcohol this once.

"You have had good practice at staying awake," I said. "I don't think I can do it."

Samuel slapped himself lightly to stay conscious. "Lost my horse in the battle above the clouds. Was serving the Tennessee army at the time. We lost two and a half times the men they did."

I stared at him as he talked. He seemed transfixed, staring into the fire as though he could see the things he described playing out there on the logs.

"We were feeling flush after our victory at Chickamauga. Brass put us up on Lookout Mountain so we could raid Yankee supply trains. They just…I think we got cocky." Samuel sniffed and poured himself a cup of brandy. He downed the cup in one go, and I was sure the story ended there.

A moment later he said, "Got separated after a bad charge. Lost one captain, then another. Horse shot out from under me. So there I was, sun was going down and I was trapped on the side of this huge mountain. Knew if I was found I was dead. You know woods are dangerous on flat land. Worse on a mountain—I could'a stumbled off a cliff or worse. Stayed put through the night sure I'd be found and killed. Kept myself awake through sheer cussedness."

Samuel shook his head and fell silent again. I stayed quiet, too. We both seemed more interested in the crackling of the fire, lost as we were in our thoughts.

"Father brought home an astronomy book for me once," I said.

Samuel glanced up at me, the shadows under his eyes seeming so much deeper for his visible sickness and exhaustion.

"I—I got up past dark when he was asleep and stayed out all night trying to find the stars and constellations in that book. He scolded me the next morning for letting the book get wet in the grass."

"You're a scholar, then." He hid a smile by leaning into the fire to light a cigarillo.

I shook my head. "Not yet. Someday. I like it, though. You tell me about all these creatures and I want to know how they work. What they're like."

“That’s easy. They’re ugly—they kill folk. Not much more to know than that.”

“But there is! You know how to hunt them, what they eat, where they like to live. They’re like animals, Samuel. They can be understood.”

“A hunter don’t need to know a deer’s favorite bible verse to put supper on the table.”

I found myself on the cusp of protest when a yawn intervened. The hour would have to be ridiculous. My head buzzed with the mere effort of staying awake. Samuel fought as well, but with liquid assistance. I caught him from time to time taking discrete sips of his flask.

“Best you get up and walk it—” Samuel was cut off by the distant boom of a gun. The sound echoed off the hills and faded into the black. I saw his hand resting on the stock of the Sharps.

I looked off into the distance toward the noise. “What was that?”

“Coach gun. Come from town.”

We both stood. I felt drawn towards the sound, and I knew Samuel did too. He craned forward like a blood hound straining at the leash. He slipped his Dance revolver from his holster and passed it to me.

“Just in case.”

At his direction we both quickly saddled and untied the horses. As soon as the straps on his were tightened he was gone, and I was not far behind. The mare danced, skittish, but I climbed into the saddle and took off after the noise—toward town. I expected for the nix to appear out of the blackness at any moment.

Chapter 20

A Stew of Your Blood

A second boom burst in town helping us find our way. A gray waft of powder smoke floating above the houses helped further. As we turned toward a familiar street a tide of knowing sickness fell over me. My sickness was confirmed when we turned another corner and saw the scene at Frau Sackoff's boarding house.

A horse thrashed on the grass, screaming its death throes. As we thundered nearer a man burst from a second story window and fell amidst a rain of glass. I could hear the fall, even from so far off.

Samuel did not even bother to stop his horse. I watched him leap from the saddle and fall to the ground in a roll. He grunted as he hit the ground and had to pause a moment to recover the Sharps rifle. He ran up the yard, clutching his side.

Lacking Samuel's experience with horses I struggled to bring mine to a stop. I did not wait to tie the mare up though, and ran after Samuel as soon as I could disentangle myself from my stirrup.

An oil lamp burned low in the parlor, casting a dim glow over the room. Even on the first floor the house felt hot, claustrophobic with wet Missouri summer air. Samuel halted ahead of me in the half light, listening. I stopped short behind him and joined. There was no sound but the whine of mosquitoes. I thought I detected the ghost of a familiar smell. My mind raced to identify it. I nearly shouted when I remembered it.

River water.

Samuel strained to peer into the dark, rifle held ready. Somewhere above us something hit the floor. I thought I heard Frau Sackoff's pained grunt just a moment before the house shook with another coach gun blast. Something up there broke. There was the sound of falling debris, tinkling glass. And then a raspy laugh.

"It's him," I whispered.

Samuel nodded and pointed at the stairs.

We took the steps as gently, quietly as we could but each board seemed to groan under our steps. The upper floors fell uncomfortably quiet, and I strained to watch Samuel entering into the deeper parts of the house's darkness. I expected him to vanish, taken suddenly by the nix's tongue.

In the stark silence I recognized the sound of bare feet pacing somewhere up there. The sound became more obvious as I crested the first flight, coming onto the second floor. Doors were open and the rooms were empty. To my relief there were no bodies. Where did the boarders go?

A deep, sharp edged voice whispered ahead of us somewhere, "Where did you go Fraulein?" There was a gleeful malice in it. Playful as a cat with a mouse. "The boy is here now."

From behind Frau Sackoff moaned, "Charlie, no!"

The nix thrust forth from the dark, teeth bared in grin or in snarl. Samuel raised the Sharps but Frau Sackoff beat him. She pulled the trigger and the room seemed to explode. Light caught the nix mid-air, burned the image in my eyes. A second later he collapsed gracelessly to the floor.

My ears throbbed painfully and the whole world sounded muffled. I thought I heard a noise and turned a little. Frau Sackoff was yelling at me, but it took me a moment to figure out what she was shouting.

"Charlie! Run, Charlie!"

Samuel yanked her out of the linen closet where she had been hiding. He pushed her at me and began shouting, "Go! Go!"

"But she shot him," I said too loud. My own voice was almost all I could hear.

He all but threw us down the stairs. "He'll be back up quick! Just go, damn you!"

Frau Sackoff and I tumbled down the stairs, I more pushed by her than willing. Above us I heard the creature giggle again

"You cannot save them from me, hunter. I will take them both and drag them under. And when they are bloated and white I will break their bones and drink the marrow."

Then I heard the Sharps fire. The creature howled as Frau Sackoff pushed me out of the house. I nearly fell over myself in the grass trying to look up to see if I could catch sight of anything. Somewhere up there I heard the sound of furniture slamming. Smaller gunfire pulled a frustrated shout from the nix. The Remington, I thought.

Then I heard Samuel cry in pain. The cry was loud and long, but at the end I heard him shout, "The camp, boy! The camp!"

Frau Sackoff hefted me into the saddle of Samuel's yellow horse. My Mare was gone, scared off by the action, but this one waited. When I was seated Frau Sackoff slapped the horse's rear and sent me galloping off into the night. When I looked over my shoulder I saw her reloading the coach gun with shells from her apron and storming back into the house.

I was two blocks gone by the time I was able to force myself to look over my shoulder. Glass exploded into the yard of the boarding house and a shape dropped. I pulled up on the reins, my heart leaping into my throat. What if that was Samuel?

The shape stirred, and I could make out inhuman proportions. It looked around, searching. And it saw me.

I whipped the reins and kicked my heels. The horse jolted forward with a start, tossing his head in irritation. Behind us the nix leapt forward eating up several feet in the process and that was enough to stir Samuel's horse. Together we bolted into the night.

My mind raced. What should I do? Where should I go? I let my finger drop to the revolver. Could I even fire it? I slipped it from my belt and looked back. He was closer now.

I squeezed the trigger. Nothing happened. Of course, I'd forget to pull the hammer back.

"Try again, little son." He giggled again and took another leap toward me.

I tried to cock the gun with my thumb but found it too firm. There would have to be another way. Taking the reins in my teeth I managed to pull the hammer back using the heel of my other hand.

I spun again and he was so much closer. I pulled that trigger. The night split in light and sound. The shot went wide and I groaned.

Ahead a house loomed large and the street came to a T. I took the left, back toward home as if by instinct. Again I took the reins in my mouth and prepared to fire. When it leapt close again I fired.

The creature hissed and stumbled backward and I gained ground. I saw him reach for his shoulder and pull the hand away, checking for blood.

"I am going to enjoy your sodden meat, Kirchner!"

I took another turn and he vanished around the corner of the smithy. Home. I had to get home. The thought came uncalled.

But why? Why did I have to go home.

The trap, of course.

I whipped the reins with one hand, holding the revolver in the other. I could lure him to the hole. I tried to buy some time by weaving Samuel's horse through the thick of town, between exposed frame houses and red brick businesses. I stormed down to the river front where lamps were lit and workers loaded cargo onto a steamer. Men shouted when I flew past them.

They shouted more when the nix landed amongst them.

My whole body shook with each movement of the horse—feeling the tremor of each hoof beat against the hard packed dirt. I could no longer tell what was the thundering of my heart and what was the thundering of the horse. We took the river road where it veered away from the river and toward home. I felt a momentary pang of regret for the dock workers, simultaneously praying that no one was hurt and that they'd bought me a few minutes.

When father's little house with its little fenced yard came into view around a bend I swung myself off the horse and smacked its haunch. The horse took the hint and made for the nearby woods. Overhead the sky grumbled, making threats of rain. I wondered how my revolver would handle that.

Just on this side of the fence our campfire still burned. I ran past it, my legs pumping as hard as they could and made for the hill. I fumbled and slipped on the incline, nearly dropping the Dance revolver.

The hole was difficult to find in the dark, hidden as it was, and I nearly stumbled into it while groping through the darkness. Slowly my eyes readjusted to the night and even simply knowing it was there stopped me from a short fall onto the spikes.

"Little Kirchner…" The voice beckoned, somewhere nearby. Apparently I had arrived just in time.

"Come to me little first born. You owe me a meal."

I sucked a deep breath and screwed up all my courage. "I do not owe you anything, monster!" With effort I cocked the six gun with the heel of my off hand.

"Such tasty marrow, such fine meat." Again he made that obscene giggle. The voice was closer now. He was not leaping, but instead waddling close. I could hear the grass shifting beneath him.

"Your great-great-great-uncle Adolphus I made into sausage."

A twig snapped somewhere to my right.

"Your great-uncle Martin I spread on my toast."

My heart skipped, and I felt I might pass out.

I could hear a sticky sound and I thought he might be licking his wide lips. "I salted your father's backstrap."

My hands shook uncontrollably and I lifted the pistol.

"I think I shall make a stew of your blood!"

He erupted from the grass on the hill above. My sluggish hands tried to raise the pistol, tried to pull the trigger. The only sound I heard was the blood thundering in my ears.

I stumbled back and he grabbed my wrist just as he landed. A powerful hand twisted my wrist at an unnatural angle. The gun fired into the night sky and silvery smoke filled the air.

A thumb-sized hole burst in the nix's chest followed by the report of a rifle. Blood spattered his body and my face. He slipped backwards and dragged me with him, surprise spreading across his slimy features.

The canopy over the hole cracked and he plunged into. His hand gripped my wrist. The air exploded from my lungs as I hit the ground at the lip of the hole, hard.

He was heavier than I, and I began to slip toward the edge of the hole. I tried to kick my toes into the ground, my fingers, anything. My wrist screamed and creaked at the pull and I felt my shoulder begin to twist the wrong way. I sobbed, fear and pain taking me as I tried to scramble back.

Footsteps pounded toward us and Samuel loomed out of the dark, the still smoking Sharps in one hand. He pulled the Remington and cocked it. A second later he put a bullet through the creature's arm. The nix plummeted the rest of the way.

The next sound of the hole was the wet squelch of all two hundred pounds of him hitting the stakes. A howl erupted from the bottom of the pit.

Samuel was at my side. He dropped the Remington and the Sharps both and pulled me away. "Charlie, you alright?"

Tears poured down my face and my throat felt raw. My wrist felt like fire burning and glass cutting. I tried to breathe, but my body would have none of it. I shuddered and gasped for an eternity before air finally filled my lungs. But to my credit I nodded.

And to Samuel's credit he did not believe me. He pulled me aside and lay me in the grass, checking the wrist. His fingers felt like knives where he probed but he shook his head. "It ain't broke." It was relief that filled his voice.

With that good news I curled in on it, wanting nothing but to pass out. "Is it dead?"

Samuel spat. He moved to the side of the pit and peered over. I noticed when he moved that it was carefully, pained. He held his side now that his hands were empty.

"Did the stitches rip?" I asked.

He shook his head. From in the pit the nix cursed and hurled vile curses at Samuel. I shrank back but he seemed unfazed. He even laughed.

"Slimy bastard's pegged on the stakes."

I pushed myself up with my good hand now, taking a limping step forward. Samuel held out a hand, though, keeping me back.

"Don't want you near him. He's still got that tongue."

"What do we do?"

"Catch our breath. Then I kill him, quick."

The nix hissed and cursed from the bottom of the pit. Every shift of his body was punctuated by a loud crunch or squelch as he further impaled himself just to get at us.

"I will let the fish peck at your rotted meat, Kirchner!" Though I could not see him the awful sounds of his thrashing made bile rise in my throat.

"I will wear your skull to Sunday mass! I will build a cage out of your bones to keep your children! You are dead, Kirchner. Dead!"

Samuel stroked his beard thoughtfully. "On the other hand we could just pump a few more iron slugs in him and let the poison finish him slowly."

The nix gurgled from within the pit.

We turned and began to walk away. I clutched my injured wrist close. The skin felt puffy and warm and I winced whenever I touched it. Already I could feel the creature's repulsive blood drying on my face despite best attempts to wipe it off. When it was safe to be near water again I would take the longest hottest bath.

Overhead the early morning sky rumbled. Samuel collected the Sharps and began to run a brush through it, preparing to load a fresh cartridge. "Won't be good for many more shots. The iron slug tears things up."

Between cleaning out the barrel and loading a new cartridge he took a nip of his pocket flask. I fixed him with a sour look but he stared back, defiant. I broke first, dropping my eyes to my bad wrist.

A single drop of rain fell on my cheek. I looked up. The sky had lightened by an almost imperceptible degree showing a thick tower of cloud cover. As I looked up a second drop slapped across my forehead. From the pit the nix began to giggle again.

A third drop was followed with a four, and a fifth. And then it was coming too quick to count. A light rain began to patter against the grass.

"Shit, shit, shit," Samuel muttered, trying to stuff the paper cartridge into the rifle. He slapped the rifle shut again and marched for the pit. Just as Samuel reached the edge and sighted down into it the giggling stopped.

"He's gone!" Samuel shouted.

My heart thudded. "Gone? Where can he go! He was staked to the ground!"

Samuel began to turn. "It's the water. The water, it's—"

A green arm reached out of thin air and hooked me around the neck.

Samuel shouted, "Charlie! No!"

Rain fell harder and the arm tensed around my neck. The nix appeared in full behind me, smelling like river water, algae, and fish decay. His tongue ran up the back of my neck and through my hair, stickiness pulling at it.

"Tell him to get back," the nix said.

I swallowed.

"Tell him!"

"What's he saying, Charlie?" Samuel called.

"He wants you to get back."

"Good boy. You have family overseas, do you know that? I think I will visit them when this is over and inform them of the breach of contract. They will be dead within a week of your end."

The nix began to drag me backwards. He braced his other wet, rot-smelling hand against the side of my head and pressed. I knew if Samuel made a wrong move he would twist and it would be over.

I sucked in a shuddering breath. “Samuel—Samuel help me!”

The nix’s grip tightened. “Silence, mewling sheep.” He continued to drag me back down the hill toward the house, toward the river.

The picture came, unbidden, of the nix dragging my father’s lifeless body to the river. A fire lit in my belly, fury replaced fear. I took a deep breath, flexed my neck against his arm.

“Shoot him, Samuel!”

The nix shouted, in crude-sounding English. “Fire and he dies!”

Samuel hesitated—then he lifted the Sharps. My hopes lifted with it. Even if I died, so did the creature.

I felt the nix tense, closed my eyes and commended myself to the God of my father. Instead of gunfire I heard the sticky sound of the nix’s maw open, felt wind rush past my face. I opened my eyes again.

The nix’s tongue crossed the gulf between Samuel and us as fast as a bullet and snatched the Sharps from his grasp. He released his grip, letting the Sharps spin through the rain and wet grass to land behind us and laughed.

“You have killed him,” the nix taunted again in German. He began to twist my head to the side.

Samuel pulled his Remington instead.

The bullet caught the Nix across the side of the head, passed through the brain pan. Stunned, he stumbled back and released me.

Samuel continued to march downhill, gun up, and I scrambled out of the way. Every two seconds he fired. The ratchet of the hammer always followed.

Click, fire.

Click, fire.

Click, fire.

Four more bullets hammered home into the beast's chest, across his shoulders, and shattered his jaw.

I fell to one side, my hands scrambling through the grass and mud searching. The rain began to fall heavier now, and even as I watched the creature's skin began to close up everywhere except the two places where the Sharps had struck. He hissed at Samuel and turned sideways as if to leave. I saw him begin to walk through the rain—*into* the rain. We would lose him again.

My hands fell on what I sought. The cold, trustworthy weight of father's old rifle. As the nix escaped I raised it and pulled the hammer back. And I fired.

The rifle bucked hard in my hands, and I felt something snap in my wrist. In the smoke cloud of the Sharp's discharge I did not see the creature fall. In the ringing of my ears after the powder burst I could not hear it. But fall he did. Three iron slugs in him, he finally collapsed and I collapsed after him.

I fell to my knees, dropping the rifle in the sodden grass, clutching my wrist. It throbbed fire. When the smoke cleared I finally saw the body.

Samuel was down off the hill in a heartbeat's passing. Without pausing he pulled an axe from near our campfire and rushed the creature. I saw the nix's hand raise if only for a moment before the axe fell.

Chapter 21

Black Sunday

The nix squealed and thrashed when the axe came down. Samuel raised it and brought it down once more and the noise ceased. On the third swing of the axe so did the thrashing. He roughly kicked something—the head I think—hard, sending it flying away from the body.

I found I felt none of the remorse over the death that I had felt for Ginny. I was glad of it. The adrenaline drained from my body at once and all I could feel was my exhaustion and my kaleidoscope of hurts.

Samuel collapsed on the grass beside me and despite the rain he pulled off his hat and began to fan himself. We sat for a while in the rain, in the thick humid air, in a silence born of exhaustion and companionship. I felt myself relaxing for the first time in months.

"We should at least get in the house," he said. He clambered to his feet and reached out a hand for me. I took it with my good hand, letting him haul me to my feet

"You did good. That was a hell of a shot."

"It was luck," I said numbly. My mind wouldn't process much. I continued to clutch my hurt hand to my chest.

He took that hand and began to probe it gently. "Sometimes luck is all we've got. Still not broken—good."

We turned toward the broken shadow of my house and started for it. As we walked I suddenly felt an iced chill pass through me.

"Someone walk over your grave?" Samuel asked. His breath misted when he spoke it. He noticed at the same time as I, and only had a moment to mutter a curse before he gripped his side and howled.

"Samuel!" I grabbed him as he fell to the ground and turned him over. His face had gone white and I could see his lips quickly turning blue. My hands were wet, though I couldn't tell how much of that was the rain. When I looked down at his abdomen I could see black spreading over it, even in the dark. Through the shirt I could feel his heat, though. He was burning, temperature swiftly rising.

A voice sounded behind us. "Samuel Henry Clayton, you are a *beast* of a man, darling." The voice echoed, sounded somehow not wholly there. I turned my head, still trying to cradle Samuel close, but he pushed away trying to sit up.

An immaterial form hovered over the body of the nix. Her clothes were white rags and her form ended just past the hips. The flyaway scraps of her rotting dress fluttered in a breeze we did not see, unaffected by the rain. And I knew her face, even with her cloudy, puss filled eyes and decaying skin: Ginny Catskill.

"That circle she drew on me. Some kind of death spell," Samuel muttered. I could not quite hear the next two words, but I thought I knew what he said.

"Witch's ghost."

She came no closer, but instead lowered to the body of the nix, caressing it with a skeletal hand. The air above it shimmered, and I realized that something was becoming visible to us. A kind of foul green mist rising off of it. The ghost began to breath in those fumes, and with each breath she became more present, more real.

Samuel tried to struggle out of my arms, to push himself to his feet. "Get the lilac. Have to stop her—she's feeding off the nix."

"Ghosts can do that?" I asked, incredulous.

He shrugged.

I let go of him and he wobbled just a bit, but still stood. His hand clutched his side as if holding his insides in. I turned for the horse, but had only taken maybe three steps when Ginny straightened. The green vapor was gone, and she was practically glowing now. Her form radiated pale white light, illuminating the dark yard as though it were early evening.

She threw her head back and spoke. I could not recognize the content of the words, but I could feel the message in my bones. She was calling to something. Mist rose off the ground shapes began to rise from that.

"No, no…Charlie!" Samuel barked. "The lilac!" He took an unsure step back as the shapes began to resolve themselves into vaguely human forms.

I lit out. The run up the hill was unsteady. Water came down in sheets and I slipped onto my knees or belly several times, clutching my throbbing hand close. The mist below me had formed into a nightmare menagerie of undead forms. Men in Confederate uniforms, women, children, business men, farmers black and white. I thought I recognized Samson among them. Each of them looked rotted or desiccated—obliterated and sent to the next world.

She howled then. "Look, Samuel! I brought friends. Behold the nightmares that haunt you every night!" Mist collected, more shapes began to form. It was an army appearing around her—an army converging on Samuel.

The yellow horse waited under the sprawling canopy of a cottonwood. He looked soaked and miserable. He nipped irritably at me when I ran up beside, but left me alone as I began to riffle through the bag. There, beneath the field kit with the needles and cat gut, were the bundles of lilac I had collected.

I had one in hand and just about ran out from beneath the tree when I realized, "These won't light in the rain." I hesitated, looking between the bundle in hand and the glowing shapes at the bottom of the hill. The sun was coming up now, though the only way you could tell in that rain was that the thick cloud cover was becoming lighter and the terrain more distinct. I ran back to the horse and fished through the bags looking for anything to help.

"Flint and tinder? Ground is too wet. What about matches…matches…" I cursed. "Samuel carries his own matches. The campfire?"

I looked down the hill. One of the dead forms, a woman in the crumbling remains of a gingham dress, walked over the fire and extinguished the last of the glowing coals with her passing. I cursed again.

"What can I do?" I asked the horse.

In the distance toward town the bells of St. George began to ring Sunday mass—and a wild idea struck me.

I gripped the saddle horn with my good hand and pulled myself onto the horse. He balked, but did not complain after more than a moment. I turned him toward the house and the army of specters and nudged the horse into motion.

Samuel was surrounded by the time we came off the hill. The horse tossed his head as we passed into and through the misty figures, snorting clouds of white in the suddenly cold air. I reached down a hand and Samuel took it, pulling himself up into the saddle.

"Ride," he said. His voice was a quiet kind of misery and he slumped against me, feeling hot and feverish.

The horse and I complied, galloping toward town. Behind us Ginny lit up with a banshee wail.

Hermann was waking. The soft rain subdued everything, and even those families leaving their houses for church seemed quiet. We drew a score of curious looks as we flew past them.

St. George was close to the heart of town, perched on another hill. It was a building of red brick and quiet solemnity. As we rode up to it I saw that the tall double doors were shut—service was begun. I helped Samuel out of the saddle and started to drag him with me toward the doors.

A wind whipped the rain around us, carrying with it the specter of a wordless cry. She was coming.

At the door I started pounding. Samuel was quiet now, eyes closed. He leaned hard on my shoulder, and I realized there was a foul smell beneath his normal scent. The stab wound must have gone bad.

A townsman opened the door, brows furrowed and prepared to upbraid the fool interrupting mass. I pushed past him before he could say anything. Samuel slung over my arm I walked up the carpeted center aisle shouting for help.

"Help! You have to help us!"

The entire sanctuary stared at us. The priest in his white robes especially—a short bald man whose eyes bulged with indignation.

“We’re pursued,” I said. “And my companion here—he’s—”

“Demons!” the man at the door shouted. He jerked the door shut and the boom of it echoed, silencing everything and everyone. He came running up beside us. “Father Staude, an army of demons is at the door!”

The congregation burst into dull roar of conversation made worse by the way sound echoed off the vaulted ceiling. Some men argued, some men wailed in fear. Others laughed or nudged their companions smiling at a private joke. The man beside me continued to implore people to listen to him.

“Dozens of them! Hundreds! All corpse-looking and dead of eyes!”

The priest raised his hands in an effort to silence his flock, but they wouldn’t have it. Nothing else to do, he took up his crook and began to pound the butt of it against the tiled floor. It just added one more noise to the mass.

Outside Ginny screamed her banshee lungs again, and that’s when silence finally returned. All that was left was the door man’s indignant, “I *tried* to tell you.”

“What is the meaning of this?” the priest asked as he stormed down the aisle toward us. His white robes swished with every step, nearly twisting around his legs.

“My friend Samuel—he’s being assaulted by these ghosts or whatever they are.” I jerked my head in Samuel’s direction. “He’s sick, too.”

The priest felt at Samuel’s white, sweating brow. “Mother Mary, he’s hot! Clear a pew, gentlemen! Clear out. We need to lay this man down. Doctor Feist?”

A man in a black suit and clutching a derby hat stood from the crowd and rushed over. "Coming, Father."

We laid Samuel out on a pew and I pulled up his shirt to show them the stab wound. "He was stabbed here. I tried to stitch up the wound several times but the ghost kept cutting the stitches."

Doctor Feist gave me a curious look. "Well…I can certainly confirm that the wound has been stitched over several times."

I withered under his brief inspection. Quietly, shamefully I offered, "I tried to pass the needle through old holes when I did it."

After a brief pause he said, "You thought well to do that. You are—were Florian's son, yes?"

"That's right, Doctor."

He nodded. "I am sorry about what happened to your father. He came to me to talk about sending you to medical school."

I could not meet his eyes. I turned my gaze back to Samuel in order to keep from seeing his pitying gaze. I was done with pity.

The priest took me by the shoulders and turned me to face him. He knelt down to my level so he could look me in the eyes and addressed me with a stern face. "What is it at our doors? What have you brought down upon us?"

"They're—it's—" I swallowed to clear my clenched throat. "There was a witch."

Those near to us gasped, and I heard whispers carry my tale to the rest of the congregation.

"Her name was Ginny Catskill and she was using her power to kill men who were hurting her friends.

She…Samuel had to kill her to set things right. Something happened and her power was turning her wicked so—so…so he killed her. Now she's come back to hurt him."

I couldn't read his face. I could not tell if he believed me or if he was on the cusp of throwing us out into the weather.

The doctor broke in. "I don't know about ghosts, father, but I know this man's wound has gone bad. He'll die if it isn't treated."

Outside the church came the moans of a hundred lost souls. And behind them, louder than the rest, came Ginny's voice. It was a high, reedy sound that might almost be confused for the wind whistling through a crack. It called out, "Saaaaaaaaaaaamuel!" beckoning like a child asking a friend to come out and play.

"Why did you bring this man here?" the priest asked me.

"He's…I was told he could help me. My father wasn't killed by wild animals. There was something out there looking for us and I was told Samuel could help with those kinds of problems."

Several nearby people made the sign of the cross.

"Did he help?" a man asked. He looked familiar, perhaps someone father worked with.

I nodded. "We killed the creature this morning. You can still find its body at my house when this is over."

Another round of gasps sparked up around me. I heard more than one voice whisper "demons," or "cursed."

The priest frowned. "That is an…interesting tale. But that is not what I asked. I meant why did you bring him *here?*"

I shifted, looking down at my feet sheepishly. "I'd once heard Catholic priests can cast out demons and Lutheran priests can't. I thought—well…I thought maybe it worked for witch ghosts, too. And the church. It's named for the dragon slayer, right?"

The congregation looked to the priest. He stood again, rubbing at a crick in his back. He was portly, and he looked tired and harried. I began to wonder if perhaps I had made a mistake.

"Your father—he worked for the winery, yes?"

I nodded.

"They have done good work for us. The love they put into their product is evident when I serve the Eucharist."

I frowned, beginning to wonder where he was going with this.

He nodded to himself. "Yes, we named this church after the famed dragon slayer. I have studied these services, but have never had to perform them. But I will help you. Your father was a good man."

"Thank you, father."

A flurry of furious pounding came on the doors. The sound echoed in the sanctuary again silencing the congregation. All of us stared at those great doors as they rattled and shook, wondering when the creatures would enter. When they could come for us.

The father stepped toward the doors, the crowd parting around him. "They will not enter this building. We are on hallowed ground and no evil can walk within."

He pointed at two acolytes, boys younger than me in white frocks. "Bring the censer and my Bible."

As I watched the priest march for the door I perceived beside me the doctor leaning in to listen to something Samuel was saying. I turned to see Samuel whispering into the man's ear.

"What is he saying?" I asked.

The doctor seemed flustered. "I'm not sure I buy into all this."

"*What is he saying?*" My voice was too high, too thin. To my mind I sounded like a hysterical child.

The man seemed taken aback. "He said—he says that the ghost is linked to him. It should only hurt him. I think he's delirious. You don't believe this, do you?"

I stepped up about to say something when the man who had taken us in spoke up. "You did not see them, doctor. They were not human."

The doctor looked away, shamed by the belief of his fellow man. "It is not rational."

"But it's real," the door man said.

"He said something else," I said.

Outside the wails of the dead rose, audible now through the doors. Shivers ran through the crowd and I heard the sound of no few men, women, and children weeping or praying.

The doctor blanched at the noise, reaching for the rosary around his neck. "We need to trap this witch ghost but I would not know how."

I frowned, thinking. Something sparked in my memory, a page from Samuel's book. Finally I nodded.

"I know what we need, but it's outside," I said. "I'll get it."

"You'll be killed!" someone said.

"I do not think so." I shook my head. "Samuel said they would harm no one but him. And even if they could, I do not think they would hurt me specifically."

I looked around at the men and women around me. No one else volunteered. Of course not. I knew they wouldn't though, for a brief second, I had hoped. The doorman escorted me to the narthex and the great doors and peeked outside.

"The rain's let up at least."

"That's something."

"I'm closing the door behind you."

"I understand."

I took a deep breath and stared at the door. His hand tightened on the iron handle and I felt my spine straighten. As sunlight cracked through I braced myself as if diving into cool water and bolted forward. Out of the dark church, into the light.

Chapter 22

Bones and Moonstones

My breath misted and my hair rose as I plunged into daylight. Chaos filled the air. A great host of men and women, soldiers and children surrounded St. George. Their arms raised and grasping, cavalry swords flashed, spectral guns fired. Figures pulled at their skin, peeling it off while others tore thin clumps of dead hair out of their own scalps.

They saw me as I saw them, and before I could even sight the horse they began to converge on me. I ducked swinging fists and grasping rictus claws. Some spat ichor and hatred while others charged me. A woman in a bridal veil and rotted white dress screamed at me, demanding to know why I had let her die, oh Jesus why.

I twisted around the shape of a hulking man in a confederate uniform, and around another with a snare drum hung from his hips, each reaching for me. And then ahead of me by a man with a long curving saber blocked my way. He was already swinging by the time I saw him and there was no stopping it.

I threw my arms before my face. I felt the blade strike me, but there was no steel. A cold sensation passed my body and visions flashed in my eyes.

The man was whole and living, astride a mighty brown horse with a broad chest. *The captain died in that last charge*, he said. *Then we shall die as well*, the others said. *No*, the man said. *I will take up the charge. We will win the day*. The other men seemed hesitant, scared. They had faced death together over and over, and eventually it had worn their souls to splinters.

But then from the back one of the men, Samuel Clayton, nodded and said *I will follow you, Captain*. This gave spine to the others, and one by one they agreed. The man, now the new Captain, led the charge. And he died, split in half by a Yankee cannon ball.

The vision fled me as the sword passed through me and I halted short, choking on air. These men, these women and children. They were all people who had died because of Samuel? Or were they people he'd failed?

The cavalry captain was coming back for me again with a powerful overhead stroke. I did not give him a chance to show me his fate again. I twisted around him and bolted. Now the horse was in sight, past the crowd. They ignored him, which was well for me.

I crossed the remainder of the church yard to where the horse waited. A mist formed between the horse and I, and Ginny formed out of the mist. She looked much as she had the last time I'd seen her—hungry, lean, feral. Not at all the smiling and jovial beauty that had first greeted me only a few days prior to that. Emboldened by the spectral army's failure to harm me I continued forward.

"Charlie, what are you doing?" Her eyes glittered, alternately reminding me of the nix and the Tiger's. They were not Ginny Catskill's eyes.

I passed through her, shivering as my body ran frigid in that small space. "I'm helping Samuel."

Her mouth turned downward, a sad frown imploring me not to. "Why?"

"Because he's a good person."

Her voice was wispy, almost immaterial. The only color to be seen in her at all was the red blossoms where Samuel had stabbed her. "No—he isn't. I've seen inside him, I've seen his nightmares. If you knew the people he'd left to die or that he'd killed himself. If you only knew, Charlie."

I hesitated, not quite looking her in her cloudy dead eyes. "He's…he had reasons for it."

"He is a bad, bad man, Charlie."

"Then he is a bad man who helps people."

Her hair flared up and her voice raised to manic pitch. "He killed me, Charlie!"

I spun on her shouting right back, "Because you were killing folk, too! You became a monster, Ginny!"

She swiftly contracted in on herself, became a tendril of smoke, quickly snaking away from me at the sound of my voice. I shivered, the sight of her burned into my mind. I could still see the rotted death snarl on her face as I began to dig through the saddlebags. The betrayed, accusing tone of her voice followed me even as I found what I came for.

I hefted out a jar of fine, shifting grey powder. It looked like the ash scrapings of any stove or fire place, but it glittered faintly in the dim morning light. What kind of bones was this made of? Whose bones was this made of?

With the jar in hand I began the trek back to the church. As I ran for the building I saw the army of specters converge on the doors. Where they massed against it white flame flared into being, burning them away. Ginny flew above them all in a whirl of tattered cloth screaming her frustration at her army.

I held the powder high, hoping they could see me from the church.

"I have the stuff!" I shouted above the din.

As I waited a few figures broke away from the crowd and came for me. I danced and dodged around them, though the woman with three great rents in her torso managed to grab me for a moment. In that moment I saw the flash of her death. Samuel stood over her killer, gun smoking, but the damage was done. She drowned in her own blood, laying in the sand of the Pecos' north bank.

I gasped as I pulled away from her, feeling like I'd surfaced from ice water. The man took the opportunity to punch at me. His fist passed through my skull, but I still had his nightmare forced upon me. *He'd been dragged into the woods by a Woman in White* (whatever *that* was) *looking for the man that killed her*, Samuel said. He pursued them into the woods and sent the Woman in White onto the next world but never did find the body of the man.

A thought surfaced as I again ripped myself out of that nightmare: how many people had Samuel saved by killing that creature at the Pecos? How many for the Woman in White?

I danced a few steps away from them and shouted again, "I have the bone powder! Help!"

Ginny rose higher, cresting before the broad circle of stained glass above the double doors. A green mist appeared in her hands and she sang. Her voice pierced my ears and froze the specters. The sound made me want to upend my stomach, or to curl up and cry.

And then the window shattered. A rain of a hundred thousand colored knives poured onto the grass. Inside I could hear the anguished, terrified screams of the congregation. She turned to give me one triumphant grin over her shoulder and flew to the window.

Even at the window she crashed against some kind of wall. Ginny strained against it, howled and pounded her fists. Each time she struck or brushed it white flame burned her. The specters below began to burn under that same white flame, several figures spontaneously bursting, crumbling away like dried parchment.

Her mist-clad hands gripped whatever the barrier was and her arms began to strain. To my horror she ripped wide the barrier, cackling, and flew in. Behind her the rest of the specters began to burn out of existence. Inside the congregation continued to scream. The double doors burst wide and congregants began to spill out into the wet Sunday morning.

I took the opportunity presented and pushed through the crowd, running back in. Inside, Samuel had been dragged to the altar by the doctor and the priest and I could see a handful of men hiding by the pulpit. The priest held high a crucifix, shouting Godly admonitions at Ginny's ghost.

"…Et Spiritus Sancti! Vade retro Satana!"

Ginny laughed, wheeling about in the air. When she passed an iron chandelier she gripped it and violently spun it. Taking another turn she raked her hands against the red brick, leaving burning red scores.

"Give me the devil in your midst and I will leave you forever, priest." Her voice sounded to me more than ever like the Tiger's that night in the Minnesota woods.

"Vade retro Satana!" the father shouted again, thrusting the crucifix into the air.

Behind him Samuel leaned against the door man. His skin was blanched white now, and purple underscored his red eyes. He saw me and snapped his fingers, pointing to Ginny. He mouthed something I couldn't make out.

Ginny howled and clenched her burning hands. Samuel screamed and collapsed to the floor, gripping his side.

"I could do it!" she shouted. "I could kill you right now!"

"Jesus Christ," Samuel croaked. "Stop bragging and just do it." His eyes flicked from me to her, and I understood what it was he wanted.

As she passed one of the pillars holding the ceiling I threw the jar. Time seemed to freeze. She turned, drawn by the motion, and we both watched the glass spiral up and out. The lid sprung free, spilling ash out in great whirlwinds, splashing against her. The jar passed clear through her, leaving ash within.

And then it shattered on the pillar. Bone ash, grey and sparkling, exploded into a great cloud. The effect was gripping and immediate. She clutched herself and fell to the ground, suddenly physical. With more weight than I'd have granted a ghost and ash she smashed through a row of pews, sending up clouds of dust.

Ginny began to struggle to rise again. Before she could get the chance I vaulted at her. I landed elbow first, driving her back to the shattered tiles.

She screamed, thrashed, gripped my hurt wrist and twisted. Pain clouded my vision, but I held my ground. I clutched around her neck, smearing bone ash on the both of us.

Then the priest joined the fray. He was there, pressing the crucifix to her brow, shouting more admonitions.

"Father, It is not working!" the doorman shouted.

"She's not the devil," I added.

The priest drew back, eyes wide and panting. He seemed to think over those words for a moment and vanished back behind the altar. A moment later he came back with a bottle of wine in one hand and a tray in the other. The Eucharist, I realized

Ginny clawed at me, twisted my wrist. We screamed together, I in pain and her in frustration. Finally she threw me off and I tumbled into the aisle. She dove for the priest next.

The doorman fell between them, grasping her at the wrists. She shoved hard against him and I saw his arms trembling under her terrible strength. They struggled, quivering, silent. Ash and a thick gummy white smoke rose off of her as she snarled and fought.

"Help us," I called to the men behind the pulpit. "We need help!"

They looked to us, to the ghost, and to Samuel.

Samuel shuddered, forcing up the effort to speak. "Going to let yourselves be outshone by a boy?"

That clinched it. They rose as one from their hiding place and joined the fray. One came in behind the doorman, pushing against him. The other took her by the neck and began to press.

Ginny thrashed, wailed, but collapsed under the weight of them. They pressed down on her, holding her at the wrists and legs. Every time she blinked I saw her eyes alternate between Tiger and nix. The effect of it caused bile to curdle in my gut.

"Do it, Father!" the door man shouted.

Timidly the priest came to her and knelt. "Do you have anything to confess?" he asked in English for her.

She spat. "Your mother was a whore—I'd know!"

"That is a no, then," he muttered in Rhinelander.

He anointed her brow with oil, making the sign of the cross with his thumb. The oil struck a soft fire where it touched her, sizzling. She shied away, wailing.

The priest looked up at us. "I cannot administer the Eucharist if she is not willing and repentant."

"Just do—" one of the men stopped to grunt as she nearly threw him off, "Just do what you can."

She gnashed and bit at him as he took her by the head and he began to pray. Ginny tried to kick, tried to hit. She bucked and thrashed, throwing up great clouds of ash and dust. The priest's voice rose, spinning out Latin in long florid sentences. Again he traced the cross on her brow and again it burned and popped against her.

Sweat beaded on his brow, dripped. If you'd asked me then, I would have sworn I saw a halo about him. To everyone's surprise, his perhaps most of all, his hands were suffused in a soft warm glow. The light struck her, eyes wide, and for a brief moment I thought I saw some remaining vestige of the Ginny Catskill I had met.

She screamed, a high wordless cry one last time and vanished into the ether. Bone ash was all that was left.

Behind us, against the altar, blood seemed to have returned to Samuel's face. "What did you do?" he asked, flushed and looking as if he'd run ten miles.

The priest backed away from the ash pile, wiping his brow. Wet ash and soot smeared his brow and stained his robes. “I tried the last rites—the Viaticum. Failing her sincere contrition, I performed the prayers for the dead.” He looked to Samuel, tired. “I commended her soul to God Almighty.”

Outside, beyond the wide open doors, soft rain pattered on the flagstones leading to the church. Thunder rumbled, muted in the distance, the storm announcing its passing.

Chapter 23

A Beginning

It was July before I could make use of my hand again. It was August before Doctor Feist gave Samuel the permission for travel. He found me one morning at Frau Sackoff's boarding house chopping firewood. I was stripped of my shirt and already slicked with sweat on account of the awful, wet Missouri heat.

Without a word he stripped his own coat, hat, and shirt and took the axe from my hands. He was still wasted and thin from his bedrest and, as we worked, I saw that the gnarled bright pink scar in his side was not the only scar he bore. All over his chest and his back I saw the traces of his professions. Puckered dots where bullets had passed, sharp triangular knife wounds, the long parallel strokes of claws.

At the end of the pile of logs I went to the water pump and came back with a tumbler of water for him. He rested, one hand on the axe, the other bringing the cup to his mouth, and drank noisily and gratefully.

"Feels good to do honest work again," he said.

The corner of my mouth twitched up. "You don't strike me as the type to lay about."

"Not the first time I had to."

I stared at the woods, not able to look at him. Likewise, he seemed to inspect the boarding house.

"You seen what they did to your house?"

I nodded. "It happened the week after the exorcism. While I'm in the boarding house no one will touch me, but that didn't stop them from torching the house."

He nodded and took another swallow of water, eyes betraying nothing. "Sounds about right. That's all the thanks you can expect for this job."

"Father Staude visits once a week, though," I offered.

"That Catholic priest?"

"He brings me books and plays checkers with me every Saturday."

Another pause. Samuel said nothing. I thought about the looks the other Hermanners had given me when father died. The looks they gave me now. "There's—there's nothing left for me here, is there?"

"Folk scare easy."

"But you still help them."

He picked up his shirt and began fanning the dirt off of it. Even stripped of his shirt, even doing menial wood cutting, he'd still worn the gun rig and the Remington at his side—still walked as though ready to draw it. There were more than physical scars on him. I stared at the thick pink line of Ginny's knife stab.

He'd taken that knife for me.

"Told you I don't help people. I'm always too late."

I shook my head. "Those specters weren't the ghosts of people you failed. They were your own nightmares brought to life. When they touched me I—" I paused, not sure how to say this. "I saw…things. I saw hunts and deaths. They were all from your perspective. They were *your* nightmares."

He eyed me thoughtfully, calculating. "Might be."

"You *do* help people. How many people would die from these creatures if you weren't around?" I stabbed a thumb in my own chest. "I know of one at least."

He nodded, looking down. He picked up his jacket and began to fish through the pockets, going for the flask. He paused, taking his hand out, and instead reached for the case of cigarillos.

I frowned. "Did you run out of brandy?"

"Something like that," he said and changed the topic. "It's a hard life."

I nodded.

"You're a sharp kid. You could still go to medical school. Become a doctor."

"Maybe."

Samuel grunted and began lit the cigarillo. He puffed, staring into the smoke, reflecting.

"Why do you do it?" I asked.

He stared into the smoke as though looking for an answer. "Because no one should see what I seen."

I balled my fists and took a step closer. "I'm the same, Samuel. I've seen it, I know what's out there. I can't go back." When he said nothing I looked down. "Besides—I have nowhere else to go."

That stopped him. The cigarillo sat perched between his thumb and forefinger. He stared at it, never looking at me.

"You're a sharp kid," he said. "You learn quick."

My heart beat at my ribs.

"Could be I could teach you a thing or two about hunting."

I leapt into the air, pumping my fists. I whooped for joy and hopped around him, screaming elation. Frau Sackoff poked her head out the back door, frowning at me. She saw Samuel and I and smiled, ducking back into the house.

"You'll do it? You'll really let me travel with you?"

He gave a one note laugh. “Better than letting you kill yourself doing it alone.”

I came to a stop before him, panting, grinning as hard as I’d ever grinned. “What do we do first? Where do we go?”

“First you finish your chores for Missus Sackoff. We leave first light.”

“Where?”

“Charlotte. Need to introduce you to some friends.”

Preview
The Dragon Lord's Secretary
By Nicole Petit

A special preview of Nicole Petit's debut novel, The Dragon Lord's Secretary, available now from 18thWall Productions

Dear Mr. Great and Glorious Dragon Lord,

I am applying for a position you don't know that you need filled, that of your secretary. Before you reject this application, please consider the following. Who organizes and polishes your treasure hoard? Dragon claws are too large and imprecise. You require an applicant with thumbs. Who organizes your schedule? Dragons are too self-interested for this work. You require an applicant willing to write down your every meeting and make sure each one fits neatly into your calendar.

I believe I am this applicant.

I come highly recommended, and I would gladly direct you to my previous employers. Unfortunately, most of them have died. Not through any misfortune or anything caused by me. They died of old age, as mortals tend to do. If you would like confirmation of my abilities, please contact Mr. Winston Churchill. He lives at 28 Hyde Park Gate, London, England, Mortal Realm.

I have enclosed my resume. It is very long. See the attached. (Inside the box. The huge box. You can't miss it.)

Sincerely,

Miss Scarlet Chase

Chapter 1

Deep in the land where magic hides, in the court of the Dragon Lord, a war as old as Camelot raged. Down past the caverns carved by dwarven hands, laced with streams of gold, fire blazed and armor clashed. Past the cavern halls smoke smudged the tableau. It seeped, black and riotous, from the mouths of slain guards. Roars shook the roots of the mountain.

In the throne room, a Knight brandished his shield against the mighty Dragon Lord.

Gales of wind from great black wings beat against the small body of the Knight. A wave of his hand and the mighty winds turned, slamming with greater force against the dragon's great head. The beast snarled, unveiling rows of sharp teeth.

"**SUCH MAGIC DOES NOT IMPRESS ME, CHILD OF THE WIND.**"

Each rumbling word beat the Knight's armor; the force of sound slammed against his ribs.

"That was no magic, lizard. That was a warning. I've killed two of your kind today. Release your captive and you won't be the third."

The Dragon Lord circled the Knight. "**WARNINGS CARRY MORE WEIGHT WHEN YOU HOLD MORE THAN A SHIELD TO COWER BEHIND.**"

The golden blade attached to his whip-tail sliced through the shield and the power of its protective runes. The Knight howled, arm shattered by the force of the blow. The floor heaved beneath him as the dragon moved forward, each step causing tremors in the cave.

The jewel hung around the Dragon Lord's neck flared through the smoke. The massive gem was said to contain the flame of the very first dragon, a power more ancient than the entirety of the Knight's own race. The Dragon Lord towered over the fallen Knight, opening his jaws wide to call forth the ancient flame buried deep in his chest.

CRACK!

A whip made of the wind sliced through the roof of the Dragon Lord's mouth. Blood quenched the fire. The Dragon Lord reared back from his prey.

"Weight only burdens you, lead scales."

Blood continued to choke the Dragon Lord, but the fury boiling in his molten gold eyes said enough. Gold claws shot toward the Knight's chest. The Knight pulled back his whip and. . .

"I swear I leave the room for one hour and the whole place goes to pot."

From the secret tunnels behind the Dragon's Throne a young lady appeared. Curls of strawberry blonde hair escaped the tight bun and bounced across a pair of black rimmed glasses. Eyes the tangly green of spanish moss peered over the rims of her glasses. With a steady rhythm she tapped a pen against a notepad resting in one arm. The Dragon Lord stepped forward, his bloodied mouth hanging open. She gasped, resting the pen against her lips.

"Lord Almighty!"

The dragon smiled, his voice almost a purr. "Yes, Miss Chase?"

"Not *you*. The *merciful* one. Come down here, let me see." She crooked a finger. The dragon lowered his head, resting it against the floor. One slitted pupil kept a close watch on the Knight. The lady leaned in between his teeth, peering up at the wound. As she prodded experimentally with her pen the dragon writhed and snarled.

The Knight brandished his whip, "Step back, m'lady. I'll set you free from this beast."

Miss Chase pulled back, making notes on her notepad. "Beast is a horrible slur. It would be proper to call the Great and Glorious Dragon Lord Calix by his name, which just so happens to be the Great and Glorious Dragon Lord Calix. What, exactly, makes you think I need to be freed?"

The Knight stepped forward, laying a hand on her shoulder. His voice softened. "You're his slave."

She grimaced at the creases his armor made against her green blouse. With distaste she brushed off his heavy hand.

"Slave? Sir, I'm his secretary."

Chapter 2

"And then you have a meeting with the Elder Wyrms For Wyvern Equality at three."

"**LEVIATHAN BURN IT ALL! NOT THOSE WALKING CASES OF SCALE ROT.**"

Heaps of gold shuddered under the force of Calix's bellow. Priceless and highly breakable objects tumbled from their piles. The secretary sighed as she walked beside him, struggling to keep her hair in its bun as the wind whipped up by the Knight grew wilder and wilder.

"Would you mind taking this fight elsewhere? I *just* alphabetized the dwarven artifacts."

"**PRIORITIES, MISS CHASE! MY KINGDOM IS IN PERIL!**" A burst of flame scorched Calix's collection of Dragon-proof armor. He fled into the deeper reaches of the Dragon Lord's hoard. Calix chased after to be met with a crack of the whip against his muzzle. He roared, and a furious lash of his tail cast an entire pile of gold into the air. A flick of the secretary's wrist and the gold hung in the air.

Miss Chase arched a brow. "Peril? A single mage?"

"**YES, PERIL! YOU LET ONE PEST IN AND AN INFESTATION IS SURE TO FOLLOW.**" He leaned down close and cleared his throat. "This would all be much easier if you would just let me eat him."

Miss Chase lowered her hand, the gold fell back into a neat pile. "Or, you know, I could just use my—"

"**NO. I'M THE HOST, HE'S MY UNWANTED GUEST. I'LL DEAL WITH HIM, NOT YOU.**" With a lash of his wings the Dragon Lord slid off, scattering treasures as he went. Miss Chase sighed and made herself as comfortable as she could in a particularly rickety golden throne. The cavern shuddered. Gales of wind knocked over her carefully arranged vases, and plumes of fire displaced her organization. Dabbing the tip of her finger against her tongue she flipped through the pages on her notepad.

"Make it quick, my lord. You have a board meeting in an hour."

"BOARD MEETING? HELLHOUNDS TAKE YOU AND YOUR STRANGE PHRASEOLOGY, SECRETARY!"

A furious roar, a scattering of gold, and the Knight was launched high into the air by a swat from Calix's claws. His tail twitched merrily, molten gold eyes glittering at the sight. Instead of the clatter of armor against floor Calix expected, he was met with a furious blast of magic. Not the wind he had come to expect, but a more dazzling sort of shockwave that could only come from…

Miss Chase yelped and rushed through the thin paths, stopping at the section she reserved for cursed items. She came to a shield of some long forgotten race (knocked woefully out of place) and stopped. It was metallic with a milky white gloss, and shaped like a chrysalis' wing. Much too delicate for its purpose. Miss Chase stared at it, tracing the thin lines with her eyes. These lines pulsed with a silver light that she never recalled being there before. Confronted with a strange new glow in the cursed items section of Calix's hoard, she did what any self-respecting secretary would. She tapped on it with her pen.

The shield quivered, the lights pulsed bright. "IN THE NAME OF ALL THE OLD GODS OF ATLANTIS, WHERE AM I? WHAT HAVE YOU DONE TO ME, BEAST?"

Calix threw back his head and laughed, drowning out the Knight's cries. Miss Chase gave a resigned sigh, adding a note at the very bottom of her to-do list:

Free Knight from cursed treasure.

Preview
The Door of Eternal Night
By Josh Reynolds

The horrifying February release in 18thWall Productions' The Science of Deduction

In the heady days of the Jazz Age, Sherlock Holmes has retired to his bees. But other, stranger detectives watch London in his absence.

Chief among them is Charles St. Cyprian, the current Royal Occultist and heir to a tradition reaching back to Elizabethan England. He, along with his apprentice Ebe Gallowglass, protect the Empire and sundry from That Which Man Was Not Meant to Know—including vampires, ghosts, werewolves, ogres, fairies, boggarts and the occasional worm of unusual size.

Tonight, St. Cyprian's night out has been interrupted by two very important men, Harry Houdini and Sir Arthur Conan Doyle. The escapist and spook-buster has a problem—a spook haunting his hotel room, a spook he can't quite bust. And it seems this particularly ghost has a bearing on a case Sherlock Holmes failed to solve, and may solve yet, if St. Cyprian doesn't untangle the mystery first.

CHAPTER ONE

The Knight and The Magician

"It was all a dream, of course. Or so I thought, at the time," Harry Houdini said, as he finished his story. "What else could it be?" He sat back in his chair, crossing his legs. "Anyway, I apologize for disturbing you, Mr. St. Cyprian—but Arthur was damn insistent."

Houdini gestured to the big, elderly man who sat perched on the edge of the nearby Chesterfield, his thick fingers knotted together. He had a large, bushy moustache and kindly eyes, which were nonetheless brimming with exasperation. "And with good reason, whatever you might think, Harry," Sir Arthur Conan Doyle rumbled. "But Mr. St. Cyprian is the expert—why not let him come to his own conclusions?"

In contrast to the angular Houdini and the hearty Conan Doyle, Charles St. Cyprian was a slim man of olive complexion dressed in one of the finest modern sartorial creations to ever emerge from the depths of a Savile Row tailors' shop. He had been preparing for a long-overdue evening out when his guests had arrived and insisted on speaking, despite the lack of appointment. But when an internationally recognized stage magician and the biographer of the world's foremost consulting detective showed up at one's doorstep, demanding attention, one had best brew a cuppa or three and settle in for a chat, regardless of social niceties.

St. Cyprian took a sip of his tea and said, "Thank you, Sir Arthur. Might I ask what makes you think it was a dream, Mr. Houdini?"

"Call me Harry. And because I don't believe in spooks, Mr. St. Cyprian," Houdini said. "But I believe in fools who do, no offense, Arthur."

Conan Doyle frowned. "None taken, Harry."

Houdini smiled thinly. "He's a bad liar, isn't he?" He slapped his knees. "It's a trick, plain and simple. Someone's having a chuckle at my expense—well, I won't stand for it. I've never yet been rooked by a phony spirit, and I don't intend to start now."

"No, well, we wouldn't want that, would we?" St. Cyprian put aside his cup and saucer. He glanced at Conan Doyle. "You disagree, Sir Arthur?"

"Most certainly," Conan Doyle said, stiffly. "I know psychic phenomena when I see it, sir. Indeed, I have seen much that science would be hard-pressed to explain. What of that Australian fellow, a psychometrist of some note, who traced the whereabouts of a missing man after touching his boot? Police forces in Europe and America call in specialists on baffling cases regularly." He leaned forward and tapped the side of his nose. "Indeed, I'm planning a trip to Australia and New Zealand in a few months to speak on that very matter."

"Of course you are," Houdini said.

Conan Doyle glared at him. "One day, Harry, I will make you see that the world is not simply a puzzle to be solved. Your own abilities…"

"Tricks, Arthur. Hokum. Legerdemain." Houdini gestured sharply. "I keep telling you—why don't you believe me?"

Conan Doyle fell silent, and St. Cyprian felt a moment of sympathy for the great man. Sir Arthur had lost a child in the War, as had countless others. And like many, he had turned to spiritualism, seeking comfort from and explanation for that grievous loss. St. Cyprian knew better than most that there were precious few answers to be found from the dead…only more questions, or worse. And sometimes, it was best for all concerned if those questions never came to light. Such was the responsibility of the Royal Occultist.

Formed during the reign of Elizabeth the First, the office of Royal Occultist was charged with the investigation, organization and occasional suppression of That Which Man Was Not Meant to Know—including vampires, ghosts, werewolves, ogres, fairies, boggarts and the occasional worm of unusual size—by order of the King (or Queen), for the good of the British Empire. Beginning with the diligent amateur Dr. John Dee, the office had passed through a succession of hands, some worthy, some otherwise, culminating, for the moment, in the year 1920 with one Charles St. Cyprian. He leaned forward.

"If you would be so kind, talk me through it again, Mr. Houdini—Harry," he asked. As he spoke, he idly clinked together the trio of strange rings that adorned his fingers. Each of the rings was inscribed with a series of characters that might have been Cyrillic or Hebrew or something else entirely. He wasn't entirely sure what they did, even now, but every Royal Occultist since Dee had worn them and it seemed less than wise to break with the tradition.

"Why? So you can convince me nothing is something?" Houdini said. "Look at this place." He gestured airily to their surroundings. The house at 427 Cheyne Walk was a perk of the job and had been since the Regency. Placed perfectly on Victoria Embankment to watch over certain old structures long hidden by the Thames, the house was unassuming, blending perfectly with its surroundings, at least from the outside. Inside, pictures of former bearers of the office lined the walls of the sitting room, jostling for space with fetish masks and lurid artworks by Goya and Blake. Great bookshelves groaned beneath a library of occult works, as well as a century's worth of accumulated bric-a-brac. On the mantle of the large, Restoration era fireplace, grisly statuary glared morosely at the visitors. "Whatever your title, you're as bad as Arthur."

"Technically, I'm a good bit worse," St. Cyprian said. "Humor me, if you would."

Houdini sighed theatrically. "It's your dime." He spread his hands. "Mrs. Houdini and I—my wife, Wilhelmina, I mean—are staying at Claridge's. You know it?"

"I've had the pleasure of Mr. Carte's hospitality, yes," St. Cyprian said.

Houdini nodded. "Swanky joint, if you can afford it. Anyway, Mrs. Houdini and I were getting ready for bed, when I felt something." He paused. "You ever get the creeps, Mr. St. Cyprian?"

"Charles, please. And yes, quite often."

Houdini smiled. "I bet you do, living in a place like this, Charley."

St. Cyprian raised an eyebrow at the familiarity, but said nothing. Houdini was a showman—he liked getting a rise out of people, one way or another. "You felt something," he said. "A change in temperature, perhaps?"

"Yeah. Pretty standard, when someone's trying to fake a phantom. Ice under the floorboards, crack in a window, that sort of thing."

"But not in this case," St. Cyprian said.

Houdini frowned. "I'll figure it out."

"Only a fool distrusts the evidence of his own senses," Conan Doyle said. "Especially senses like yours, Harry."

"Flattery aside, senses are easy to fool. That's practically my bread and butter, Arthur," Houdini said, rolling his eyes.

"Exactly!" Conan Doyle slapped his knee. "And who better to know if he was being fooled. That you can't, implies that you aren't."

"Or that it's a new, more subtle form of trick," St. Cyprian murmured.

Houdini gestured. "See? Even your ghost-breaker pal agrees with me!"

Before Conan Doyle could argue further, St. Cyprian said, "I neither agree nor disagree. In my experience, things are rarely what they seem. Further investigation is called for. What happened next?"

Houdini was silent for a moment. Then, at a nudge from Conan Doyle, he said, "I saw a guy…a real swell gent. Old fashioned though. Worse than Arthur here."

"I beg your pardon," Conan Doyle blustered.

"Apology accepted," Houdini said. "Didn't look like a spook. More like a banker. Only…" he hesitated again.

St. Cyprian sat back. He fished a silver cigarette case out of his jacket and popped it open. He took one of the hand-rolled cigarettes out and popped it into his mouth while he waited for Houdini to finish. "Only what?" he pressed, as he proffered the case to his guests.

"Hand-rolled. An oriental blend?" Conan Doyle said, waving the offer aside. Houdini shook his head, frowning.

"A Moro woman of my acquaintance," St. Cyprian said, as he slid the case back in his jacket. He touched an index finger to the tip of the cigarette, and puffed gently. A thin tendril of smoke rose as he shook his finger. Houdini glared at him.

"That supposed to impress me, Charley?"

"Is what supposed to impress you?" St. Cyprian said. "Now…you were saying? What about this banker so perturbed you?"

"Besides the fact that he was in my room in the middle of the night?"

"Besides that, yes," St. Cyprian said, smiling slightly.

"He was…missing something." Houdini tapped his chest. "Didn't look like he gave it up willingly either." He swallowed. "It was red. Like it was on fire, and I could see…" He trailed off. "I could see everything that wasn't there," he said, finally.

St. Cyprian took a drag on his cigarette. "And then?"

"He said something. Only I couldn't make it out. It was like he was under water, or far away. It was just noise. Then he was gone." Houdini snapped his fingers. "Like a soap bubble popping. Damndest thing." He shook his head. "I'd pay good money to know how it was done. I could use a trick like that in my act."

"Unless it wasn't a trick," Conan Doyle said.

They began to bicker again, and St. Cyprian excused himself. He stood and wandered towards the fireplace, thinking. It could have been a trick. He'd seen such before, and Houdini was a ripe target for such a ploy—the famous medium-buster, busted at last. It would garner headlines, if nothing else. Houdini would be ruined, or, at least severely embarrassed. Spiritualists and seers the world over would sigh in relief.

"But it doesn't feel like a trick," he murmured, watching the fire.

"Holmes used to talk to himself. He said it was the only way he could be certain of a good conversation," Conan Doyle said. St. Cyprian turned. The other man stood behind him, hands clasped behind his back. Houdini still sat in his chair, frowning at nothing in particular. Their arguments were quick things, brief spurts of heat, quickly snuffed.

"Did you ever take offense?"

"What would have been the point?" Conan Doyle said, with a shrug. "Watson endured more than I ever did. He had to live with him, after all." He paused. Then, "I...was sorry to hear about Thomas. He was a good man. Much like my own...my Kingsley."

"Yes," St. Cyprian said, stirring the fire with the poker.

"Did you ever...I mean, I know you and Carnacki were all over, but, did you..." Conan Doyle began, hesitantly.

"We never had the pleasure, no," St. Cyprian said. "I'm sorry."

Conan Doyle waved a hand. "Do not apologize." He looked at Houdini. "In any event, we are not here to reminisce about a life lost, but to save another."

"You think this spirit means Houdini harm, then?"

"Quite the contrary—I think it was attempting to warn him," Conan Doyle said fervently.

"Your chum Holmes ran across something similar in late 1899 or thereabouts," St. Cyprian said, scratching his chin. "Carnacki was just starting out, then. Holmes approached him during an investigation...something to do with a chap named Phillimore and a brolly?"

Conan Doyle nodded vigorously. "I remember that.

Watson spoke of it once or twice. The tale of Mr. James Phillimore, who, stepping back into his house to get his umbrella, was never more seen in this world," he said, with an air of recitation. He shook his head. "John claimed to have written about it, but it's still locked up tight in that tin dispatch box of his, so I've never seen it."

St. Cyprian nodded. "I only know some of it. Supposedly Phillimore, like our Mr. Houdini, had the misfortune to meet a ghostly harbinger...unfortunately, its warnings fell on deaf ears. Or simply came too late. Phillimore was gone a few days later, never to be seen again." He continued to stir the fire, thinking.

"Holmes never spoke of a ghost," Conan Doyle said.

"No, I rather think he wouldn't have. Holmes was convinced that it was trick and Thomas already had a reputation, much like Mr. Houdini's, for outing fraudulent mystics." St. Cyprian stepped back, frowning slightly, the poker resting on his shoulder. "They never figured it out. Or so Thomas claimed. A few months later, Holmes became preoccupied with another case—some beastly business in Ipswich—and Thomas took up his duties as Edwin Drood's apprentice." He heard the door slam. "And speaking of apprentices..."

"I got him," a young woman's voice crowed. "Right where you said he'd be, too. Cheeky bugger. Had to hit him with a—oh. Guests, is it?" she said, as she came into the sitting room, dragging a heavy roll of purple cloth. Somewhere, a church was missing its altar cloth, St. Cyprian suspected.

The newcomer was dark and slightly feral looking, with black hair cut in a razor-edged bob and a battered flat cap resting high on her head. She wore a man's clothes, hemmed for a woman of her small stature, beneath a heavy convoy coat that had seen better decades. There was something dark splattered on both the coat and her trousers, and she'd tracked more of whatever it was in across the floor. Conan Doyle and Houdini stared at her, and she stared back.

She let the roll of cloth flop heavily to the floor. There was something unpleasant wrapped in its stained folds, and it groaned softly, until Gallowglass gave it a swift kick. "Should have figured we had guests, if you were still here." She grinned at St. Cyprian. "What'd she say when you begged off, then?"

"What did who say?" St. Cyprian said.

"Whichever dolly-bird you were seeing tonight.' She looked at Houdini and Conan Doyle. "Sometimes they throw things at him. One of them sent him a scorpion in the post once."

"I say...a real one?" Conan Doyle said. He looked at St. Cyprian speculatively.

"Gentlemen, my apprentice, Miss Ebe Gallowglass. Late of Cairo, currently of Kensington. Miss Gallowglass, may I introduce Sir Arthur Conan Doyle and his good friend, Mr. Harry Houdini?" St. Cyprian said quickly.

"Ey up," Gallowglass said. She shot St. Cyprian a look. "I'm his assistant."

"That's what I said," St. Cyprian protested.

"What's in the bag?" Houdini said.

Gallowglass shrugged. "Bogey."

"A bogey?" Conan Doyle said, eyes wide. He seemed to have forgotten about the scorpion, thankfully.

"What's a bogey?" Houdini said.

"It's what's in the bag," Gallowglass said, pushing her cap back up on her head. She looked at St. Cyprian. "Want me to...*kchkk*?" She drew her thumb across her throat.

'No. Put him in that devil-box we brought back from Lewes last month. I daresay that'll keep the perisher quiet until we can figure out what to do with him," St. Cyprian said. "And then come back down. We have work to do."

"Joy," Gallowglass said. She grabbed the edges of the cloth and began to drag it towards the stairs. St. Cyprian winced each time whatever was inside bumped on the steps. He looked apologetically at his guests.

"She's really quite handy."

"A modern woman, by the looks of her," Conan Doyle said.

"Was she dragging a man up the stairs?" Houdini said. "I could swear I heard that carpet groan." He stared after Gallowglass, his expression puzzled and a bit apprehensive.

"Not a man, no," St. Cyprian said. "An unwelcome tenant, soon to be transported elsewhere. I'd like to see your room, if I might. At Claridge's, I mean."

"I've already checked it," Houdini said, still looking at the stairs.

"Nonetheless," St. Cyprian said. He tossed the remains of his cigarette into the fireplace. "Think of it as a second opinion, if you will. A fresh set of eyes."

Houdini traded glances with Conan Doyle, and sighed. "Fine. Like I said, it's your dime, Charley. It's your dime."

"Excellent!" St. Cyprian said. He rubbed his hands together in glee. "Now, let's go have a chat with this ghost of yours."

CHAPTER TWO

MRS. HOUDINI

Claridge's sat snugly at the corner of Brook Street and Davies Street, in Mayfair. The hotel had flourished in the wake of the War as displaced aristocrats of all nationalities sought a suitable London residence. Supposedly, the deposed and exceedingly maudlin king of Ruritania lived at Claridge's when he wasn't serving as the doorman at Barribault's.

"Swanky sort of place, innit," Ebe Gallowglass said, as they followed Houdini and Conan Doyle inside. The foyer was a thing of columns and a floor of alternating black and white tiles. A chandelier hung at its centre and there was a curving set of stairs to their right. "Nicer than the Savoy. Wonder if they got a beastie in the basement as well."

"I shouldn't think so. And I'll ask you to be on your best behaviour, Miss Gallowglass," St. Cyprian said. "No raiding the bar, no threatening the guests, no unlimbering that artillery piece you call a pistol, *if you please.*"

"What—this?" Gallowglass said, pulling back the edge of her coat to reveal the heavy shape of the Webley-Fosbery revolver holstered beneath her arm. "Self-defense, innit?"

"I doubt we're going to be attacked by anything more dangerous than snide commentary in here, so hands off," he said firmly. His assistant had the distressing habit of seeing problems as a nail, and herself as a hammer. It was one he was trying his damndest to break her of.

If she lived long enough, Gallowglass would have his job, and be welcome to it, given that he'd likely be dead. Few Royal Occultists lived to collect a pension, though more than one had defied the odds to die alone, unsung, and unremembered at an unseemly age in a debtor's prison or a hospice ward. He liked to think he'd make it long enough to write his memoirs, but he doubted it. There was a reason Carnacki had allowed that fellow Dodgson—or was it Hodgson?—to write about him for *The Idler*, after all.

Perhaps that was why the Great Detective had allowed Conan Doyle to record his cases. St. Cyprian wondered whether the man had been slyly pleased at the publicity, even as he made a show of disdaining it. Perhaps Holmes had been, at heart, a showman, much like Houdini. *Too bad I can't ask him.* Holmes had, by all accounts, retired to Sussex at the end of the War, to enjoy his dotage and bees.

Thinking of Holmes made him recall the case of James Phillimore. Carnacki had been assiduous about keeping records. Dodgson's stories had been sanitized for public consumption, either by the writer or Carnacki himself. But the records told the unvarnished truth. Somewhere in the dozens of moleskin notebooks which littered the desk in his study was a record of the events pertaining to that case. As he and the others followed Houdini up the stairs, St. Cyprian wondered if he should dig the notes on the Phillimore case out.

The Houdinis had taken a suite on the third floor, with windows looking out over Brook Street, and the rows of terraced houses which lined it. Houdini didn't bother to knock, before flinging the door wide, to reveal a large sitting room, occupied by couches, chairs, and a fine piano which sat opposite a modest fireplace. Sumptuous rugs were spread protectively across the hardwood floors, and a small chandelier hung over the centre of the room.

St. Cyprian stopped as he came in, senses prickling. He cast a quick glance around, but saw nothing. Nonetheless, he felt it. There was something here, and yet...not. He could almost hear it. Like the hiss of a Victrola with its needle askew. His palms were suddenly sweaty. He felt Conan Doyle grip his elbow. "You feel something, don't you Charles?"

"Something, yes. I can't say exactly what, however."

"I've returned, sweetheart mine," Houdini said, throwing out his arms and puffing his chest. "Come and greet our guests, Mrs. Houdini." A thin, seemingly frail woman ducked under his arm and took Conan Doyle's hands.

"Arthur, you dear man. It's been ages," she said, ignoring Houdini.

Conan Doyle laughed and bent so that she could kiss his cheek. "Mrs. Houdini, as ever you are the light in the darkness."

"And what am I? Chopped liver?" Houdini protested.

"Wilhelmina, but you can call me Bess," Mrs. Houdini said, extending a pale hand towards St. Cyprian. "I don't believe we've been introduced. Are you a friend of Arthur's? He said he was taking Mr. Houdini to meet a spiritualist of some sort, only you don't look like a fraud at all."

"Bess," Houdini said, almost plaintively.

"Looks can be deceiving," Gallowglass said, pushing

past St. Cyprian. Hands in her pockets, she slouched towards the suite's liquor cabinet. A bottle of something red was already out, and sampled. "Who wants a drink?"

Bess watched the young woman pounce on the potables, and then glanced at her husband. "Have we adopted an alley cat, Mr. Houdini?"

"Mine, I'm afraid. I apologize for Miss Gallowglass' lack of social graces. Her talents lie in stranger vales than that of politesse. And I am Charles St. Cyprian. Neither spiritualist, nor fraud, though I know a bit about both."

"A pleasure to meet you, Mr. St. Cyprian. Arthur says you're the man to see about ghosts and such," Mrs. Houdini said. She smiled as she said it. From what he'd read, Bess Houdini was no less a sceptic than her husband, albeit a more genial one. For Houdini, it was a war. For Mrs. Houdini, it was a minor disagreement.

"I am indeed," St. Cyprian said. "Would you mind showing us where the spectre in question made its appearance?"

"Right to it, then?" Mrs. Houdini said, bemused. "I thought you English-types liked small talk."

"Ordinarily, I would be at your disposal, but your husband seemed most insistent that we get this over and done with as quickly as possible."

"Like I said on the way over, Charley...we've got a show tonight, for a private audience. They want to see the Great Houdini up close and personal. Who am I to deny them such a rare opportunity?" Houdini said. He pointed. "It was in the bedroom. Mrs. Houdini?"

"Follow me," Bess said.

She led them to a large bedroom, which was set off to

the side of the sitting room. Its windows were on the same side, and he could see the glow of the street lights through them. A large four-poster bed occupied most of the space, and a rolled up carpet leaned against one wall.

"I checked every inch of this room after our guest vanished," Houdini said, leaning against the door frame. "No hidden wire, no holes in the ceiling, walls, or floor. I was tempted to peel the wallpaper, but I'm already spending enough dough on this joint without adding a bill for damages in."

The sensation St. Cyprian had felt upon entering the suite was stronger here. It emanated from nowhere in particular, or perhaps everywhere. Something from Outside had come in, and it still had its foot in the door. There was a sort of miasma to these things, a creeping odour of the intangible. He traded a glance with Gallowglass, who nodded.

"Yeah," she said. She felt it as well.

He gestured, and she nodded. She sank to her haunches near the bed and extracted a mouldering satchel from her coat pocket. Strange sigils were stitched onto the satchel. She plucked a piece of chalk from it.

"You want to do the honours, or you want me to do it?" she asked, bouncing the satchel on her palm.

"You're the one with the artist's touch. Keep it neat, though. Remember what happened in Lewes, what?"

"That wasn't my fault," Gallowglass said sourly. "The floor were wonky." She extracted several short sections of polished wood and began to assemble them into something resembling a snooker cue. Once it was complete, she attached the chalk to the tip and began to scratch out a circle around them. As she did so, she murmured the words to a certain incantation, crafted by Dr. Dee himself for situations such as these.

While Gallowglass drew the protective pentacle, St. Cyprian reached into his coat pocket, feeling through the various amulets and charms which he carried with him at all times. One never knew when one might need an Assyrian demon-whistle, or a silver coin blessed by the Anti-Pope of Avignon, and it was best to have them close to hand, just in case. His fingers closed on the bottle of Hyssop oil, and he extracted it, giving it a deft shake as he did so.

"Medicine oil?" Houdini said, as he eyed the vial.

"Hyssop," Conan Doyle said, confidently. "A purifying agent."

"Very observant, Sir Arthur," St. Cyprian said as, thumb over the top of the vial, he began to sprinkle the oil around the interior of the circle. "It can also be used to protect those seeking to commune with the spirits."

"Bushwa," Houdini coughed into his fist.

St. Cyprian smiled serenely. "Quite possibly. I do know it's more effective on some occasions than others. Ghosts are rather like a...spiritual fungus, if you will. Some of them are more resistant than your average spook."

"Spiritual fungus," Houdini repeated. "Far cry from the usual line, I admit. What do you think, Arthur? Still backing your boy's play?"

"Despite the inelegance of the description, I have no argument with it," Conan Doyle said stiffly. Mrs. Houdini laid a hand on his arm and frowned at her husband.

"Mr. Houdini, I'll ask you to stop baiting poor Sir

Arthur. He's trying to help, as you well know." She smiled prettily at Houdini. "And since you seem stumped, what say we let them give it a try, hunh?"

"Spiritual fungus," Houdini said again, as if that answered her question.

"If I'm not mistaken, you admitted to believing in psychic phenomena of some kinds, didn't you, Mr. Houdini?" St. Cyprian said, not looking at the magician.

"I thought I asked you to call me Harry?"

"Forgive me," St. Cyprian said. "Harry then—telekinesis, ectoplasm, that sort of thing?"

"I offered cash for proof, if that's what you're getting at," Houdini said. "Maybe there's something there, maybe not, but I've yet to see any evidence."

St. Cyprian said nothing. If Houdini wanted proof, he could stick around. Then, some minds were like fortresses. Nothing of the spirit world could penetrate their psychic defences, or not permanently at any rate. Mostly they saw nothing at all, and what they did see, they soon forgot or rationalized. Houdini was the latter sort, he suspected. His mental equilibrium was enviable, as was his spiritual fortitude.

Gallowglass was of a similar cut. There was something about her which put off the more ethereal types, St. Cyprian had noticed. In the same way dockside roughs would cross to the other side of the street when they saw her coming towards them, ghosts, spooks and spectres would waft out of her path with unseemly haste. She rarely appeared to notice them, and when she did, she mostly ignored them, unless they were a threat.

"Will you be calling the ghost tonight?" Conan Doyle

said, breaking the moment of silence. "Are the aetheric vibrations conducive to such an attempt?"

St. Cyprian hesitated. He traded looks with Gallowglass, licked his finger and held it up. After a moment, he said, "Yes."

Conan Doyle flushed as Houdini laughed. "Are you mocking me, sir?"

"Heaven forefend, Sir Arthur. The truth of it is that ghosts have a sort of...of frequency, I guess you could say. Once they've made an appearance, all it takes is a bit of fiddling with the knob to bring them back. Quiet you," he added, as Gallowglass snickered. "Tonight would be best. The closer to the moment of its initial appearance, the stronger the signal."

"This gets better and better," Houdini said.

"Has he told you about the Thin Man yet?" Mrs. Houdini said, mildly, as she watched them make their preparations. Houdini stared at her in chagrin. She ignored him. "That gentleman who chased our car from the train station? The one who was watching us from across the street as we dined last night?"

"No, I daresay he didn't," St. Cyprian said, looking up at the magician.

"Harry—what is this? What's she talking about?" Conan Doyle said.

"It's nothing, Arthur. We get creeps like that all the time. Don't we, Mrs. Houdini?"

"No," she said, with evident good humour.

"I'm shocked, Mrs. Houdini. Shocked and appalled," Houdini protested.

"Mrs. Houdini," St. Cyprian began.

"Bess, please, Charles," Bess said, smiling at him.

St. Cyprian inclined his head. "Bess, then. Why do you call him the Thin Man?"

"Obvious reason, really. He's a bit of nothing, stretched out and fluffed up. Strange sort—haven't seen robes like that since Cairo. Taller than any Egyptian, though. Too tall, really." She hesitated. "I don't like him. He's been shadowing us since we got to London. Almost as if he's keeping an eye on us for some reason."

"Why didn't you tell me about this, Harry?" Conan Doyle said.

Houdini threw up his hands. "Why? We go through this in every town. If it's not Arabs throwing me down a hole, it's German spies trying to seal me in Bakelite. I'm famous, Arthur—there's a downside to it, as you well know." He glared at them. "Look, I got this show to do. Mrs. Houdini?"

"Everything's sorted. A motor car will be here to pick us up in a few minutes. I've got your bag, a few tricks suitable for a party—your handcuffs, that sort of thing. Gave the stage crew a night off as well, but told them to be back at the theatre at nine. Colonel Bobdillo is taking us out for dinner first, and then..."

"Bobdillo?" Conan Doyle said.

"You know him?" Houdini asked.

"I don't believe so, no. But I've heard the name perhaps. Dashed if I can remember where though," Conan Doyle said, doubtfully. Though he said nothing, St. Cyprian felt an inkling of the familiar as well...a snatch of memory, but in regards to what he couldn't say.

He rolled the name over in his head as he continued his

preparations. Something to do with Carnacki, perhaps? London was lousy with occultist of various stripes. Most were of the harmless variety—little more than antiquarians of a ghoulish bent. He knew most of them, by name at least. It paid to have a list of who'd bought what, when it came to certain outré items. He'd headed off a fair few problems that way.

Before he could say anything, someone knocked at the door to the suite. A few moments later, Houdini ushered a small, straight figure into the suite. "What are the odds? The man himself," Houdini said as the newcomer bobbed into the bedroom and turned.

"I'll allow as how my ears were burning, yes. Allow me to introduce myself—Colonel Bobdillo, Jasper to my friends, among which I hope you'll be counted," the little man said, as he took Mrs. Houdini's hand and patted it in a grandfatherly manner. His voice was a wheezy hiss. He wore a frayed overcoat, long out of fashion, and a top hat that added considerably to his meagre height. "I am most pleased to meet you, Mr. Houdini. I have long been an admirer of your exploits in the field of amateur escapology. When I saw that you would be coming once more to our fair shores, I thought it surely destiny." He glanced around, head wobbling.

Houdini preened. "Well, who am I to argue with destiny? Shall we get this show on the road? Arthur—care to join us?" He glanced at Bobdillo. "I'm sure the Colonel doesn't mind if the esteemed Sir Arthur Conan Doyle tags along."

"Mind? No, great heavens, no. The eminent author himself? The great defender of Spiritualism? Why, we'd be honoured. But what about your other friends? I don't believe that we've been introduced yet, sir," Colonel Bobdillo said, as St. Cyprian stood.

"St. Cyprian. Charles St. Cyprian," St. Cyprian said. Colonel Bobdillo didn't offer to shake hands, which was something of a relief. The little man had set his senses a quivering, and St. Cyprian felt like a hound scenting a bear. Bobdillo was definitely 'in the business' as the saying went. Though in just what capacity St. Cyprian couldn't say.

"Ah. I've heard of you. Thomas' boy-in-the-back," Colonel Bobdillo murmured. St. Cyprian blinked, uncertain of whether offense had been intended. The old man looked at the chalk circle drawn on the floorboards and quirked an eyebrow. "Thomas Carnacki, I mean. Smart chap. Bit daft, but smart. Are you a smart chap, St. Cyprian?"

Something about the way he asked the question put St. Cyprian's teeth on edge. Nonetheless, he smiled and said, "According to some."

Colonel Bobdillo smiled thinly. "Perhaps we shall put that to the test, at some future date. My card, sir," he said, presenting a thin white rectangle to St. Cyprian. As he did so, St. Cyprian noticed a tattoo on the side of his hand, nearly hidden by his thumb. Before he could see it clearly, Bobdillo retracted his hand. "Feel free to call upon me, should you wish, when you are finished with...whatever this is." He snapped his fingers and turned, spreading his arms. "But not tonight! Tonight is for a more entertaining form of magic—but first, the best meal Mayfair has to offer." He swept forward in his curious bobbing way, ushering the others out of the bedroom.

Gallowglass whistled. “Funny geezer, weren’t he?”

“Yes, quite,” St. Cyprian said, still puzzled. He looked down at the card Bobdillo had given him. It was white with Bobdillo’s name and address in Seven Dials, picked out in gold. Besides these there was a highly stylized symbol.

“Is that supposed to be Cleopatra’s Needle?” Gallowglass said, peering around his arm at the card he held. “Looks like an obelisk. Only it’s got wings.”

“Symbolism, innit,” he said, mimicking her cadence. He slid the card into his pocket. “Let’s get cracking, shall we? This ghost ain’t going to dashed well call itself forth, now is it?”

Preview
The Speckled Band
By Hannah Lackoff

The horrifying March release in 18thWall Productions' The Science of Deduction

You know the story. The whistle in the night. The crumbling mansion. The gypsy camp. The cheetah and the baboon kept wild on the grounds. The bell-pulls that lead to nowhere, and the "swamp adder" that scurries down them to attack young women. Dr. Watson described it all in the measured tone of the medical man.

But there was a story Dr. Watson did not know. A story of privation, hidden fortunes, illegitimate children, the origin of the cheetah and the baboon, and dear, lost India. This is the story of Helen Stoner.

For the third installment of The Science of Deduction, Hannah Lackoff presents a feminist gothic in the tradition of Wide Sargasso Sea. Using Sir Arthur Conan Doyle's own descriptions and dialogue, Lackoff writes the story behind one of Sherlock Holmes' most famous cases, "The Adventure of the Speckled Band."

There was a legend in our village in India, a tale of a monster designed to keep children careful in the forests, and used for all manner of things from making them adhere to a bedtime schedule to returning home at an expected time to finishing a plate of food. Mother never used it on us, but Deitur and Mahari's both did, and I had heard Grimsey threaten Julia with it on numerous occasions as she grew into a teenager and left the embassy hill to meet up with Deitur.

The description varied from family to family; sometimes it was a lizard with an angry spotted collar, sometimes a striped spider. Most often, however, it took the form of a snake. Always, it had long curved fangs and terrible breath. Sometimes it bit an arm, sometimes a leg, sometimes it would carry off whole children in its haste to wrench them from their families. We only half believed it, but it always gave us a delicious chill and made us step carefully in the woods.

The name of this creature, of course, was the Speckled Band.

We were not happy to leave India. It was all we knew and we loved it by default the way happy children care for their only home: the climate, the food, the noises, the people. It was where Papa was buried. We refused to go.

It didn't matter, of course. Mother and Grimsey said we gave them no choice, but that wasn't true. We could have stayed on our own. We had the house and the servants, and Julia of course had Deitur, and there was Moki and Anan besides. I volunteered to work with some of the older ladies down in the village, learning to sew those beautiful shawls they sold to tourists and British nationalists more gullible than we. I said I would provide for us. All of us, I said forcefully, and Julia nearly cried.

Grimsey bellowed because that was the only way he talked anymore, and said that we had no idea how much it would cost to run a place like this, and regardless the house belonged to the government, and even though these seemed like two contradictory statements Mother didn't correct him because she was too worried about keeping her marriage aged daughters eligible for society. I pointed out that Julia already had a marriage proposal that she had accepted, but no one listened. We packed our bags under protest.

The night before we left I crept into Julia's room but she was gone. I waited at her window, wrapped in her mosquito net, but she didn't come back, and I feared that I had lost her, and I wished her well.

When we were younger, when Mother and Grimsey were only courting, we were allowed to run wild. Mother was in still recovering and trying to work and she hardly noticed where we were, and he did not yet feel as though he had authority over us. We lived in the village still, and Julia and I ran and played with Deitur and Mahari and the others, taking off our English boots and hats as soon as we were out of Mother's sight. We knew the village as well as they did, and better than Mother and Grimsey.

Even when we moved to Embassy Housing on top of the hill and Grimsey made us go to the British school we still found ways to leave and return to our old village, to our schoolmates and of course to Deitur, whose father had been German but whose mother was the most beautiful Indian woman we had ever seen. We knew the roads to his house, and to Mahari's, so well that our bare feet recognized each stone on the road and root in the path, and danced on them so easily that from the time we were ten years old we hardly had to wash our feet at all to hide where we had been.

Julia should have been able to hide from Grimsey forever, but he paid his servants well and they knew the roads as completely as we did and had no loyalty to Julia or myself. When they brought her back her feet were bare and bleeding and I knew everything had gone wrong. Julia and I did not have feet that bled. Not in Malla.

Grimsey gave her to two of the new servants to bathe her. He would not let me help. He wouldn't let Mother near her. When he thought I couldn't hear he told Mother that if she could not control her children, he would. When Mother through no one could hear, she wept. We were not children. We were twenty-one years old. We were going back to England, away from Julia's disgrace, to be married off to someone pale and British and suitable. Someone Grimsey would choose.

He didn't always disapprove. That came later, when his practice began to fail and he began to drink, smuggling bottles out of the embassy bar and back home to our kitchen. Drinking made him meaner, or maybe it made him more honest. Maybe he had only been pretending to like us, had never approved of anything about us; Mother's short hair and our injured animal sanctuary, our friendships with the locals and our multilingual tongues and the way Mother made enough of a living on her own, as a woman, to fully support two growing children, even if it was only in semi-rural India. If she hadn't gotten sick, Mother never would have put up with him, but her illness, and losing Devi, and almost losing myself and Julia, changed her.

Mama met Devi when we were five. We barely remembered life without him, and we loved him, and he loved us even though we were little white semi-orphan terrors who ran the village uncontrollably. He was tall and dark and he let us climb his arms and legs and perch on his shoulders like two pale parrots. He spent the night with us often, even though that was unusual, even though it was frowned upon but both the British and the Indian villagers. He helped Mama too; when she made her rounds with her vials of medicine and her needles.

We would have called him Papa, but Mama sat us down and had a talk with us about how we had already had a Papa, and everyone only gets one. Our Papa was our Papa, and Devi was our Devi, which may have been true, but Devi died of the same fever that Papa did, and almost took the rest of us with him.

Mama sent for the Embassy doctor when she saw how bad it was, but the Embassy doctor, who we only knew at the time as Dr. Roylott, said he could only take the white people back with him. He promised to return with medicine for Devi, but either he never did or it was too late by the time he made it back down the hill, because Devi never came to stay with us again, and Mama was so sad that eventually we just stopped asking.

We were only children. We recovered quickly, but Mama did not. She was weak and she couldn't work for very long; only an hour or two at a time until her concentration left her and her muscles spasmed and she had to sit down, or sometimes lay down. We brought her fruits and nuts, we brought her our newest baby, Moki, but nothing helped. Dr. Roylott came down for a regular checkup, and eventually he became our stepfather and we moved up to the Embassy with him. Mama became Mother and stopped working. She grew her hair out. She insisted we wear shoes. We knew she missed Devi, and Papa, but Dr. Roylott seemed a poor substitute. We assumed he would die soon, like our other fathers, but Dr. Roylott must have come from stronger stock because he didn't go away.

We called him Grimsey because we thought it was funny, and because, even though he was a doctor as fastidious about hygiene as the rest of them, there were something dirty about him, something off even before he took to the bottle. Mother didn't like it, but her will had left her. She let him spend her money; the money she had earned through her clinic and the money she had left over from the settlement when Papa died. And because he was in charge of the money, he believed himself to be in charge of the household, and listened to no one's voice above his own. And so it was that when Grimsey decided it was time to return to England, we went.

The passage was rough and Julia railed against it, crying and screaming and threatening Grimsey, calling for Deitur and vomiting up everything she was given to eat. He gave her sedatives, and at first she spit them out, and later she hid them in her cheek, but after a while she accidentally swallowed some and then it was like she couldn't stop swallowing them. I don't believe she intended to kill herself, but I don't blame her for being sad. And anyway, she didn't die. She merely slept for days and days and then weeks until eventually Grimsey had to stop giving her pills so she would be able to eat.

When she woke up, we could see England. It was raining. I would learn later it was a regular occurrence, the rain, and it was different than the rain in India: colder, and harder. All of London was colder and harder, the whole of England perhaps. I lost my desire to go barefoot when I saw the state of the streets and what was thrown into them. I especially lost my desire when I saw that none of the streets led to anything but more streets.

But before that, I stood on the deck with Moki wrapped in a blanket in my arms. He was shivering too, and I stood away from the other people so they wouldn't see his little squashed face and become frightened. He didn't look at the shoreline, but I did. He buried his eyes in my brand new jacket, purchased for the trip, while I watched my new home that the rain was unable to wash into the water no matter how hard it tried.

We went below to our quarters and I returned Moki in his cage, a condition set by Grimsey. Moki hated the cage, he was seasick and so was Anan. Everyone was ill except Julia and I, but Julia hardly counted as she was asleep the whole time. Even then, Grimsey didn't let Julia be alone. It looked like love to Mother, it looked like devotion and concern, but it wasn't. Their quarters smelled and Mother moved in with the animals and me, but she didn't talk, just took some pills from Grimsey's stash and curled up to sleep on our shared cot. Moki huffed and turned his back, because when Mother was there I couldn't bolt the door and let him into the bed with me at night.

No one was happy. No one had been happy for a very long time. It's entirely possible that no one has been happy since.

Made in the USA
Lexington, KY
12 July 2017